Overnight Shift

by Bill Siracusa

Overnight Shift

Production copyright FurPlanet Productions © 2019

Text Copyright © Bill Siracusa

Illustrations and Cover Artwork by Skye 2019

Published by FurPlanet Productions
Dallas, Texas
www.FurPlanet.com

ISBN 978-1-61450-519-8

Printed in the United States of America
First Edition Trade Paperback

"DALE!" yelled a voice behind him.

Jerking violently awake, Dale Wallace realized he was in a sitting position with just enough time to avoid crashing over backwards. The cheap black office chair he was sitting in, which was probably in its 28th year of an estimated 10-year service life, tilted onto its back wheels but amazingly did not dump Dale onto the scarred pine floor.

Wide-eyed, he took a moment to realize where he was.

He was safe and sound on the second floor of the Marshall County ranger station in Kentucky, smack in the middle of four hundred acres of forest preserve. The station was built in a log cabin that was almost 120 years old, and had been adequately funded for around 40 of those years. Like any county installation, they scraped by with what they had. Dale was surrounded by ancient office equipment, 30-year-old field radios, cheap plastic folding tables, and ten-year old computers. He was working on one of these now, cataloguing donated texbooks, which was such enthralling work that he had dozed off after less than ten minutes.

Unlike most of the other rangers, Dale didn't mind the office work. Most of the team would rather have been scouting a bluff for a lost hiker or scanning the horizon for a late-summer wildfire. Not Dale. He wasn't in it for the nature—he was more in it for the solitude. Dale was 48, and this was the most remote job he'd ever had, and not-coincidentally, the one he liked the most.

He looked back to see who had yelled at him. His head hurt. His bones ached. Dale was in terrific shape for his age, short and thick and well-muscled, but his entire body hurt. It felt like the flu, or like he had lost a fight. Or like he had lost a fight with a guy who had then given him the flu.

Kate Campbell appeared next to him. She was young and pretty and smart, dark-skinned and athletic and an absolutely-gifted naturalist, and Dale had no idea why she liked him. She wore her red hair in a tight ponytail and she looked great even in the rangers' green-and-khaki uniform. "Dale, buddy. You need to go home," she said, frowning. "C'mon, I'll give you a ride. I'm about to leave."

He shook his head, trying to blink himself awake. The other rangers were heading out for the night. Dale would hold down the fort until the morning shift got in at 8:00. "I just got here," he grumbled.

Kate frowned. "Dale, you're sick as a dog. You're in no shape to be working the whole night. Especially on a double."

He shook his head, feeling light-headed. "I'm fine. Just didn't get any sleep last night." He blinked. "I'll get my second wind any minute now."

"Seems like you're sick. Do you feel like you have the flu?" She sat down in the metal folding chair next to him.

He let out a sigh. "I have no idea. It just came on this week. Hit me like a truck."

"Did you see a doctor?"

He shrugged. "Kind of. I went to one of those drugstore nurse things. Everything came back negative." He finally looked at her, frowning. "I'm fine, Katie," he grumbled.

She watched him for a moment, smiling. "Surely you've figured out by now that I'm not just going away, Daleford," she said.

"So I noticed," Dale snapped, through his teeth. It felt overly harsh the moment it came out of his mouth, but that happened to Dale a lot. Dale never knew what to say, and his anger frequently got the better of him, but for some reason Kate always knew what he meant anyway. Kate had defused several situations in the field when Dale's temper had gotten the better of him. If he was honest, she was probably the only reason he was still employed. He didn't know why she was so nice to him, but she was.

True to form, Kate just nodded knowingly. "Alright," she finally relented . "If you start to get worse, go home and go to bed, you know? Or sleep on one of the sofas. Fire season is over and it's too cold for hikers. Turn the radio volume up and sleep it off."

He considered. That was actually really good advice. "Yeah… good call," he said, quietly. "Thank you."

She frowned. "I don't know why you don't just go home. You've never taken a sick day and it's not like Adam needs the company."

Dale stiffened at the mention. He thought of the burly grunt that the county had sent to do the eletrical repairs on the station. Adam was tall, friendly, and built like a linebacker. He was a foot taller than Dale and looked like a slab of beef. Dale felt his face get warm just at the mention.

Kate looked at him and seemed to read his thoughts. "Unless… Adam is the reason you're holding out…" she said, looking away, innocently.

Dale stared at her, wide-eyed. "Nope!" he snapped. "Not interested!"

Kate's fake innocence evaporated in a moment and she turned. She raised one eyebrow, grinning. "Really? You're not the least bit interested in the charming country idiot who could lift you over his head with one massively muscular arm?" She leaned in, smiling infuriatingly.

Dale didn't look at her, and felt himself start to blush hotly. He frowned. Truthfully, Dale was interested. Dale was extremely interested. But Adam was young and friendly and looked like a construction worker who was also a model, and Dale already knew it was doomed from the start, so he had kept Adam at arm's length. Well—what Dale would consider arm's length. Most people would probably consider it "open hostility." Adam had been, to Dale's shock, entirely unphased, but he knew from experience that everyone had their limits and sooner or later Adam would get tired of him.

Frowning, the older ranger said nothing.

Kate grinned. "You know what I've always liked about you? You're an honest man, Dale," she said.

He blinked at her. "What?"

She smiled at him knowingly. "You never lie to me. You just sit there and blush." She raised herself out of her chair. "It's a refreshing trait in a man."

Dale sat and glowered.

Kate picked up a logbook on a clipboard off the desk next to him. She flipped up the top page and began to review it. "I think you should go for it. I know you like him and the big friendly labrador type is perfect for you. Could work."

Dale blushed so hard he felt his heart pounding. He really didn't like discussing the topic. "Like hell! He's been hitting on you since he got here. In case you hadn't noticed."

She shrugged. "He could still be bi. And even if he isn't, he's the type of guy who would find it flattering."

Dale narrowed his eyes. "Katie, I am old and I feel like trash… I would rather chuck myself into Silver Gorge tonight than flirt."

She took a deep breath and let out a sign. "I didn't think so. Ah well, it was worth a shot." She reached under the desk and pulled out her purse, which looked more like a small backpack. "Just don't get in a fight with him like you did with the drywall guy."

Dale wrinkled his nose. "He started that and you know it."

Kate smiled at him. "I know, I reviewed the security tapes. You gave him a pretty good run."

Dale chuckled. "Damn right I did."

Kate considered. "I think Adam could give you a run for your money, though—you would probably lose." She raised a conspiratorial eyebrow. "Unless… that's the idea?"

Dale scrunched his face up, feeling his heart pound. "Katieeeee," he grumbled. The idea resonated a little too strongly with him.

"Do you want me to talk to him for you?"

"NO," Dale said, eyes wide.

Kate smiled. "Awesome! You two can just continue having horrible miscommunications, while I watch, and neither of you listens to me, and I just sit here and quietly go insane," she finished, cheerfully.

Despite himself, Dale smiled. "That sounds great!" he grunted.

Kate waved to the last of the other rangers departing for the day. Dale half-turned his head, decided his neck was aching too much, and half-heartedly waved over his shoulder.

Kate flipped one page on the logbook, stole Dale's pen off his desk, and signed it at the bottom. "There," she said. "Reviewing that was your big job for the night. Now you can concentrate on being a good host, or sleeping for ten hours and getting paid for it."

"Mmm," Dale grunted, noncommittally.

They sat in comfortable silence for a moment. Outside in the parking lot, gravel crunched loudly.

"I think I hear Adam now," Kate said. She headed for the balcony.

Dale sighed.

***

Warm fall air poured in through his open truck door as Adam Chaney climbed out of his Marshall County work truck. The suspension creaked loudly as his considerable weight transferred onto the gravel. It was Thursday afternoon, a little after two o'clock, and the sun was still high in the sky. The air smelled like leaves and gravel dust—not too hot, not too cold—with just the right level of humidity. A perfect fall day. It would be warm and comfortable until at least eight or nine o'clock. It was beautiful.

Too bad I'll be stuck in this cabin in the woods, he thought, gazing at the work site.

Oh well. He was getting a full night's worth of overtime pay. Double-time pay was definitely worth sacrificing one fall evening, even if it was beautiful. Tomorrow he would sleep in, and next Friday he would have a nice fat paycheck. The upcoming money made it hard to complain.

Heading to the truck bed to pick up his toolbox, Adam took a moment to enjoy his surroundings. Way out here at the ranger station, set up on top of a picturesque rolling hill, all he could see for miles was rural, winding road and trees in every imaginable shade of red and yellow and orange, falling down toward the interstate and town center. It was a scene taken straight out of a tourism commercial—"Visit scenic Marshall County, Kentucky!"— except for Adam, the oversized country grunt in a dingy white t-shirt and thick khaki work pants. For a moment, all he could hear was cicadas buzzing and birds chirping, and then one of the rangers yelled at him from the second-floor deck of the ranger station.

"Break time already? Didn't you just get here?" she called down at him.

He looked up.

It was Kate Campbell. She smiled down at him from behind the dark wood railing, twelve feet over his head. Kate was in her twenties, and with ponytailed red hair and a seriously athletic body. She had caught Adam's eye as soon as he'd started the job, a little under a month ago. He had asked her out on the fourth day of the project. She had said no, but at least she'd been nice about it. In Adam's experience that was still kind of a win.

Adam crossed his big arms and frowned up at her. "Excuse me, Ranger Kate! County electricians get two breaks a day. It's not my fault the ranger union isn't pulling their weight. You guys should go on strike and let the forest burn down or something."

Kate laughed, and then her eyes left him and settled on the pile of electronic components and rubber insulation in the back of his truck. Adam had been the last employee to the county garage this morning, and thus had gotten the crap truck with the squeaky fan belt and the missing bed cap. There were three large spools of wire, and a milk crate filled with outlet boxes and tubing, which had dumped its contents out everywhere on the winding county roads, and scattered across the entire floor of the truck bed. The only thing that had stayed put was his massive toolbox, and that was only because it weighed as much as an old CRT TV.

"You got a lot of crap there, Chaney," Kate observed. "You want some help with that?""

Adam shook his head. "Naw, I got it. The toolbox is the only heavy part." He reached up and played with his short beard.

Kate smiled down. "If you say so!."

Adam smiled, and climbed slowly up onto the rear bumper of the battered white truck. He lifted one thick leg over the tailgate, and the beat-up Tacoma wiggled as he moved into the bed. Adam wasn't big so much as "hulking"—at 6'4" and 300 pounds, and more muscle than anything else—the back of the truck sagged noticeably under his weight. His hair was extremely light blonde, but he kept his head nearly-shaved anyway. He also had a close-cropped but very thick beard that was a few shades darker—dirty-blonde, almost brown. He was pretty hairy too, to an extent that an ex-girlfriend had described as "within acceptable margins, but only just," so he was used to being watched, or at the very least stared at.

While he was still gathering things, Kate stepped out the front door, a few feet away from his truck, in a short-sleeved green button-up uniform shirt and khaki shorts, with big hiking boots. He hadn't even noticed her leave the deck. "Hm. I said no, and yet here you are," he said, seductively.

She laughed. "I don't want you herniating yourself trying to impress me," she said, raising an eyebrow. "I already rejected you, so it would be pretty pointless." She watched him shove boxes along the scraped bed toward the dented tailgate and then held out her hands. "Gimmie something to carry. And not something light, either, or I will take it personally and flatten your ass right here in this parking lot."

Adam smiled. "Thanks! I hate going up and down these rickety-ass stairs. My feet barely fit on the treads. I'm just glad you didn't send down Dale." He handed her a big box of rubber couplings.

Kate looked back up toward the building, frowning. "I can handle it. Besides, he doesn't look so good. I think he might be getting the flu or something."

Adam snorted. "I think what he's got is a bad case of hating my guts."

Kate smiled angelically, balancing her load, leaning forward to pick small cases out of the bed and make a little stack. "Oh please. Dale likes you just fine. You jock boys are so sensitive. I told you, there's two reasons people become rangers—because they're really good with nature, or—"

11

"—or because they're really bad with people," Adam finished, cracking a smile. "I remember. I'm just glad you're so… kind and welcoming." He winked, setting another two long boxes on top of her pile."

Kate laughed in his face. "Oh wow, you're still trying! That's adorable. Anyway, just leave him alone tonight and you'll be fine." She frowned, backing up so Adam could jump out of the truck, hefting the load of haphazardly stacked boxes in her arms. "I still don't see why you have to finish all the electrical work tonight. Our wiring has been a train wreck since the roof leak, and that was in like… January. It's a miracle the building didn't burn down over the summer. So why the rush now? It waited ten months, but now it's urgent?"

Adam stepped over the tailgate and dropped into the parking lot, his thick construction boots raising twin size-16 clouds of dust as he crashed down into the gravel. "Because the repairs lasted a little over a month. The project was approved in the budget for this month, which ends tonight, and my boss doesn't want to have to requisition a whole new project budget for the whole month of November just so we can use one day of it."

Kate stared at him. "So your department is charging the county… what, 12 hours of time-and-a-half? Just so your boss doesn't have to fill out another form?"

Adam nodded, grinning. "It's double-time, actually. But, yeah."

Kate raised a skeptical eyebrow.

Adam shrugged, chuckling. "You know how this red tape bullshit goes. You work for the county, just like me." He reached into his truck and pulled out his toolbox. It was the biggest in the department, weighing close to sixty pounds, but for Adam it was nothing. "Besides, I like working overnights—the money is good." He cocked his head. "I'll be fine unless Ranger Dale tears my throat out. Are you sure you don't want to swap the overnight shift with him?"

Kate laughed, hefting her load up to her chest. "Oh, please!" she said. "He's just a big puppy. You'll see. In fact, why don't you…" She trailed off. She looked like she wanted to say something else, but stopped herself. "You know what, never mind. Let's head in.

She broke eye contact, leaning against the door to hold it open for him.

Adam frowned, reaching into the truck and grabbing three long pieces of conduit in one big hand. That was weird, he thought, but a moment later he had to pick his way up the narrow stairs and forgot all about it.

***

On the first level of the ranger station was the Marshall Valley Nature Center. It was two thousand square feet of prairie exhibits: cross-sections of soil composition, specimens of native bluegrass and other midwestern plants, and a dozen or so examples of museum-quality taxidermy. It had a small library and a classroom, public restrooms, and a modest gift shop. While its traffic could not compare to, say, the Marshall County Water Park, the little Nature Center did get plenty of traffic in the summer and a steady stream throughout the winter months. It was a favorite field trip destination for the four adjoining school districts, and one of the top day-trip spots in the mid-state area.

The upper level was devoted to a fully-functional firewatch and ranger station, a home base for the groundskeepers, tour guides, and naturalists that maintained the four-hundred acres of preserves. There were six full-time rangers, but they could probably have used four more, handling everything from drunken teenagers to prairie burns. But, budgets were tight, so six was what they got.

Adam saw Dale Wallace as he reached the top of the open stairwell.

"Hi, Dale," he grunted as he stepped up into the room. Most of the station was a large, open room, lined with folding tables, all of them topped with equipment, with a row of small offices along the far wall and a small kitchenette. In the corner at the top of the stairs, the rangers had set up a little waiting room, with a 70's era couch and two uncomfortable looking armchairs, all upholstered in stiff red-and-gold plaid and surrounding a long, scarred, dark-wood coffee table covered in pamphlets. The sofa faced the stairs with its back to the rest of the open area. It was a homey little touch.

Dale looked up from the ancient-looking computer he was carefully typing on with his two index fingers. He nodded at Adam impassively, dipping his chin. "Chaney," he said, a little too loudly.

Dale Wallace was a short man, probably 5'8" or less, broad-shouldered and stocky. He had a low center of gravity, and he always seemed to Adam like he was sizing him up, as if he was deciding who would win in a fight. He wasn't aggressive—nor was he particularly friendly—but he always struck Adam as vigilant. And not in a "protect the innocent" way—more like an "Am I going to have to fight you?" way.

When Adam had first met him he immediately thought ex-Army. Maybe ex-Marine? Ex-something. Dale was also pretty hot, which Adam had also noticed immediately—with his square jaw and dark black hair, it was hard not to—but he hadn't even entertained the idea of going for it with the older ranger. As hot as Dale was, Adam was quite sure that he was more likely to get socked in the jaw than score a date.

As usual, Dale watched him just a moment longer than necessary. He had started to turn back to his spreadsheet when he saw Kate coming up the stairs, with her arms full of electrical components. He did a double-take, his brown eyes widening, and looked at Adam like he was going to start growling. "You made her carry all that?" he demanded, scrambling out of his ancient plastic office chair. It did a little spin behind him. He started toward her.

"It wasn't up to him," Kate said, matching Dale's tone. "You sit back down! You're not feeling well!"

Three feet away, Dale froze in his tracks, eyes widened again. A moment later, he resigned himself to sulking. Adam had noticed early that Kate had a way with Dale that nobody else could seem to match. "Katie, I would have helped," the older ranger grunted, frowning.

As Adam tried to gently set down his toolbox, without dropping it straight through the pine floor into the Recycling and You exhibit downstairs, Kate dumped her load onto the ancient couch. "It's fine, Dale," she said. "I didn't even break a nail."

Adam held back a smile. Dale stared at both of them.

"Go sit back down!" Kate insisted, shooing Dale back toward his computer. "I'll make you some tea before I leave."

Dale shrank back, retreating toward the makeshift desk. The computer was one of two perched on a folding table, flanked by old metal file cabinets, against the interior wall of windows that adjoined the conference room. "You don't have to do that," he insisted. "I feel fine." The stocky ranger frowned, steadily backing toward his chair. "It's nothing."

"Nonsense!" Kate cried, disappearing into the little kitchenette in the corner opposite the staircase "SIT DOWN!"

She left Adam and Dale staring at one another.

Dale blinked at Adam, and went a bit red in the face. "I'm fine," he protested, though Adam hadn't asked. "Really."

Adam cracked a smile at him. "I'm sure you are. But, I think you won't be if you push it with her."

Dale stared at him, unblinking for a moment, and then he snorted, like an annoyed horse. As per usual, the conversation between them had ranged from "awkward" to "contemptuous."

"You'd better go sit down," Adam said, raising an eyebrow. "She's gonna kick your ass."

"Mmm," Dale said, narrowing his eyes, and wordlessly returned to his chair and the computer.

Blinking at the ranger's back, Adam rolled his eyes.

I guess we're done talking, he thought.

***

Twenty minutes later, Adam was ready to get to work, and Kate was about to head out for the day.

When he'd started rewiring this building a month ago, the Nature Center downstairs had been the priority, since there was a lot of exhibit lighting, and of course that was the public face of the preserve. The official reason for the repair job had been the roof leak, but as far as Adam could tell, most of the electrical "ghosts" were probably due to nothing more than old, horrible wiring. The massive cabin had been built in the 1870's, and remodeled in 1965, and most of the electrical work was frighteningly out of code.

Overnight Shift

Adam had gone through six 100' spools of wiring downstairs, and thus far, none of it had been related to the actual roof leak.

Tonight, he was finally going to tackle the short itself. Four outlets in one interior wall of the ranger station had shorted out and died nearly a year ago, taking out two PCs and a shortwave radio in the process. The station was reliant on lots of electrical equipment, and of course, having a massive ongoing electrical short in the building used to manage forest fires was not ideal. As it was, to compensate for the lack of outlets, one of the rangers had gone to Home Depot three weeks after Christmas and bought about three dozen 100' green extension cords. They ran back and forth, behind tables and across pathways, like a network of rivers.

Adam had taken a look at the damage previously—it was easy to spot, directly over a huge murky-beige spot in the tiles of the drop ceiling—and had figured he could finish it in one night. Kneeling in front of the center outlet, however, staring at a pair of telltale melted prong holes, he wasn't so sure. It looked like the entire line had fried.

Behind him, a few feet away, Kate was talking to Dale, on her way out the door.

"Now, you be nice," she said to him. "We don't want a repeat of the incident with the drywall guy."

Dale grumbled something unintelligible.

"I know," Kate said, back to him. "But, this is just one night." She turned to Adam. "And we need him if we want the lights to work," she said, smiling.

Adam looked over his shoulder and scoffed. "You don't need me for that," he said, grinning. "The lights are on a different breaker. You only need me for the outlets."

Dale frowned at him, crossing his arms. "There are plenty of outlets downstairs," he said icily.

Kate shot him a look.

Adam stared at him for a moment, and then smiled. "I'll stay out of your way tonight," he said. "You won't even know I'm here." He smiled disarmingly.

Dale frowned at him, took a deep breath, and visibly softened. "It's fine. I have some projects to work on anyway," he said.

Adam frowned. The ranger did look a little pale.

"None of that heavy lifting downstairs," Kate warned him. "That's why we have high school interns."

Dale visibly colored, his cheeks reddening under his black stubble. "Fine. Don't you have a date to get to? I'm sure this time he picked a really nice sports bar."

Kate glowered at him.

Dale swallowed and held up his hands. "Fine! Fine! Fine!" he said. "I'll take it easy." He dipped his head, looking embarrassed. Adam tried very hard to pretend not to notice.

Kate grinned. "You'd better, Dale," she said. "Or Adam is going to rat you out."

Adam froze with his hand on a screwdriver. He looked up, frowning. Kate was grinning at him. Dale was not.

He shook his shaved head. "Nuh-uh," he said. "You leave my ass out of this. I'm going to be out of here by midnight, and I ain't looking back."

***

2:31 PM

Adam was going to be there, he decided, until at least three or four in the morning.

"Shit," he hissed, under his breath.

It wasn't just the roof wiring that was fried. The connections to the outlet boxes were also all toasted. Also, almost all of the pass-throughs in the studs were too narrow and needed to be re-cut to meet code, which was a four-hour job, minimum. On top of all of that, Adam found three different sets of live wires that had simply been taped off. There wasn't even a wire nut—just electrical tape! It was a total shit-show. The water-short might've actually been a blessing, if the breaker hadn't been switched off for the last ten months, the entire ranger station could easily have burned to the ground.

As it was, there was charred wood and singed wiring just about everywhere Adam had looked. No wonder one tiny water leak had fried the entire circuit.

It was pretty clear that a non-professional electrician had done all the wiring on the interior walls. (Assuming it was an electrician at all. It could just as easily have been somebody's cousin who knew how to solder.) Nothing was up to code, the gauge was way too light for the current, and the splice into the breaker box looked like a rat's nest.

Replacing the burned-out wiring was going to take at least a couple hours, and he would probably have to follow the wiring all the way to the breaker panel. That meant going up into the attic. This was turning into a twelve-hour job, at least.

Adam sighed heavily, crouching in front of the short wall. This was going to be a pain in the ass.

Behind him, Dale cleared his throat. Adam turned.

The ranger was carrying a weathered file box full of what looked like old school textbooks. It looked heavy, and the ranger's thick biceps bunched impressively inside his button-down. Adam allowed himself to stare.

"I'm going to get started downstairs," Dale said. "We just got a bunch of donated textbooks, and I'm going to go work them into the collection."

Adam cocked his head. "Want me to carry those down for you real fast?" he asked.

Dale's eyes narrowed in anger, his mouth tightening. He started to flush.

Adam let out a sigh, closing his eyes. "That wasn't an insult. Kate said you weren't feeling well. I didn't know if you hurt your back or something."

Dale blinked at him and then deflated, cheeks coloring faintly. "Oh. Uh, right." He swallowed and shook his head. "No, back is fine. I'm just a little worn out, that's all," he said. "Anyway, I'll be in and out for a little bit, but then I'll be downstairs for a while reorganizing things. Let me know if you need anything from your truck, okay? The door locks behind you." He thought for a moment. "Did you bring something to eat?"

Adam shook his head. "I was planning on hitting McDonald's around eight or nine."

Dale cocked his head, raising an eyebrow. "I remember when I could stomach that trash." He shrugged. "Suit yourself. Just let me know when you leave because I'll have to let you back in. Doors are locked after six p.m."

Adam nodded, and then risked a half-smile. "Are you going to take it easy?"

Dale stared at him, and Adam got that peculiar sizing-up feeling again. The ranger took a long time to speak. "Are you going to rat me out?" he said, his voice dangerously low.

Adam stared back for a long moment, and then grinned. "Naw," he said.

Dale watched him. "That's it?" he asked, suspiciously. "No witty retort?" he asked. "No charming commentary?"

Adam cocked his head and sighed wearily. "Would it make a fucking difference, Dale?" he asked.

Dale stared at him for half a second, shocked, and then frowned… but not in anger. The ranger was virtually impossible to read, but just for a second Adam thought he looked a little bit… disappointed? But, then he turned away and started down the stairs. "Nope!" he called back, over his shoulder.

Adam watched him go.

This is shaping up to be a great night, he thought. At least it would be kind of cool working in a big cabin in the woods.

***

12:46 AM

Adam hated the ranger station.

Covered to his elbows in drywall dust, with an Extra Value Meal sitting unhappily in his stomach, sore, dirty, and soaked through with his own sweat, Adam hated the ranger station.

He hated the rangers, hated the building, and now, by extension, hated the abstract concept of nature itself. He wished he hadn't even discovered this horrible wiring clusterfuck, and that the entire building had burned to the ground because at this point, it would be easier just to build a new facility completely from scratch.

He was on his back, lying on the floor between two shoved-aside folding tables, arms raised over his head. He was wrist-deep in electrical guts, trying to work upside-down inside the wall because if he ripped out any more drywall then the poor carpenters would be stuck at the ranger station for just as long as he was.

Even with his clear safety goggles, there was sawdust and bits of drywall in his eyes, and he'd forgotten his damn bandana at home So now, his sweaty, bald head was coated in a thin layer of dust which had caked on and dried like cement.

Gritting his teeth, he fought with a stripped screw from underneath an outlet box, his muscular arms quivering with the effort of holding the screwdriver tight against what little groove was left in the screw, seriously entertaining the thought of just tearing the entire fucking stud out with his bare hands and starting over. His teeth hurt, he was so exhausted, his eyes stung, and he was so warm he could smell his own deodorant baking away.

There was a clatter toward the front of the building. Adam looked down his chest at the staircase, and caught Dale's eyes as he cleared the top of the staircase. The ranger had stripped off his button-up and was now dressed in a t-shirt more or less like Adam, minus the pit stains and the fine sheen of sweat.

Dale walked up to Adam's feet and cocked his head. "Thought for sure you'd be wrapping up by now," he said.

"Yeah, I thought I so, too," Adam snapped, lifting his big arms back over his head.

Dale cleared his throat and checked his watch. "You know, it's after midnight," he said. "It's almost one, in fact."

"That did not escape my attention," Adam grunted, without looking.

Dale was quiet for a moment. "Your, uh, budget only ran through the end of the night," he pointed out.

"A-yup!" Adam said, a little too loudly.

Dale cleared his throat. "So, you're working for free?" he said, puzzled.

Adam grunted unhappily. "Yeah," he said. "S'what I get for caring about stupid shit, like whether or not this building burns down!" He lined up the screwdriver again, clamping his big hand around it.

Dale was quiet for more than a few seconds, and when Adam looked back down, he found he was alone in the room again.

He sighed loudly. Whatever. If Dale really didn't want to like him, then fuck it. Adam wasn't here to make friends. He went back to the stripped screw, cursing all the rangers and their miserable old building.

Ten seconds later, he felt tapping on one of his big feet.

The screwdriver slid out of the groove, and Adam cursed loudly. "What is it, Dale?!" he demanded, looking down and gritting his teeth.

His eyes narrowed in anger, Dale was holding a pair of Miller Lites in clear glass bottles. The beers were obviously ice-cold, covered in glistening condensation, just like in the commercial. Even from four feet away Adam could sense their cold, liquidy refreshment.

They called to him.

Wide-eyed, Adam stared longingly at the bottles. "I take it all back. I'm sorry. I love you."

If Dale was amused, he didn't show it. He snorted, cocking his head. "C'mon, Chaney," he said, thumping him on the boot. "Let's take a break."

***

They walked out to the deck, where Dale sank idly into one of half a dozen armless wooden benches built into the deck. He gestured to the one across from his, and Adam obliged. The upper deck was lit at each corner by a colossal sodium-vapor light thirty feet up a telephone pole, surrounded by a cloud of white-lit flying insects, but other than that it was just the stars and the full moon.

The temperature had probably dropped into the 50's, but after marinating in his own sweat all night, Adam was perfectly comfortable. Steam actually rose off his white undershirt in a delicate fog, until a light wind picked up and whisked it all away.

"Okay," Adam said, letting out a breath. "Maybe this place isn't so bad," he said.

Dale nodded thoughtfully. "I thought you might feel that way."

Adam took a long swig of his beer, finishing off half the bottle in one long pull. He relaxed his big body in the rigid chair, tilting his head back, feeling the night and the beer leach the heat out of him, from inside and out. "I gotta say, this ranger business doesn't seem like such a bad gig."

Dale grunted, playing with the label on his bottle. "It pays the bills," he said. He finished off his beer and reached in for another.

Adam looked down into Dale's bag. There was an entire six-pack. "So, is this dinner?"

Dale shrugged. "My shift is two til eight, so technically this is lunch. You gonna judge me?"

Adam shrugged. "No sir." He raised his bottle in a toast.

Dale stared at him, and then turned away. He took a deep breath, and let it out as a long sigh, taking a pull off of his new beer.

They were silent for a few minutes.

Adam drank, and watched the bugs, and enjoyed the cool night air. He tried to be quiet, but as the beer settled into him, he felt like talking.

"So, how'd you end up here?" he asked, glanced in Dale's direction. "At the station, I mean."

Dale opened his mouth, and then closed it without responding.

Adam glanced at him. "Traumatic story?" he asked. "Or, are you just giving me the silent treatment?" He cracked a little smile.

Dale blinked at him, and let out a soft sigh. "It's not traumatic. I have a criminal record."

Adam finished his beer, choking the last of the suds down his throat, and turned to regard the ranger. "You're shitting me," he said. "For what? Jaywalking?"

Dale clenched his teeth, staring darkly at him, and Adam saw his nostrils flare. "Aggravated assault," he said.

Adam blinked at him. "Jesus Christ," he said.

Dale glanced down at Adam's big hands. "You finished your beer," he said. He looked down at his own bottle. "Here, take mine. I only had a sip." He reached forward with it, offering it neck-first like the butt of a gun.

Adam looked down at it, unmoving. "You sure?"

Dale nodded. "Yeah. Here!" He frowned, wiggling the end of it. "Ain't gonna bitecha," he said.

Adam grunted, reaching forward for the bottle. "Thanks," he said. "I hope I don't catch whatever you got. So, ah, you gonna tell me what hap-"

Dale groaned audibly. "It was at a bar. Some redneck shitbag was pushing his girlfriend around, and I didn't like it, so I told him so. He wasn't too happy. He knocked her down, probably just to spite me, and I really didn't like that. So, I rearranged his face with a pool cue."

Adam stared at him, unable to lower his eyebrows. Abruptly, he began to feel the alcohol. He'd drunk it awful fast, he concluded.

Withering under his gaze, Dale lowered his head and let out a shaky sigh.

"How long did you get?" Adam whispered.

Dale shrugged. He picked up Adam's bottle and began playing with it. "Just two years," he said. "I got out early for good behavior."

Adam took another long swig, marinating in that information. "What the fuck," he said, finally. "Seems like an awful lot for defending some rando's honor."

Dale snorted, finally cracking a smile. "You have no idea. The rand- ah, the young lady testified against me, too. Standing by her man, I suppose." He looked up. "I fucked the guy up pretty bad," he said. "He went blind in one eye."

Adam blinked at him in surprise. "I... ah... wow," he said finally.

A colossal moth began fluttering around the sodium vapor lamps above them, big enough for the flapping of its wings to be audible down on the deck. As Adam watched, something dark and black swooped down to eat it.

Dale shrugged shallowly. "Sorry you asked?"

Adam cocked his head. "Sorry for what happened to you. Sounds like a pretty raw fucking deal."

Dale let out a long sigh. "Yeah. It can really hold you back." He shrugged. "S'how I ended up out here in the middle of the fucking woods, drinking shitty beers with an annoying county worker."

Adam processed that for a moment, and then grinned. He couldn't be sure, but it looked like Dale was hiding a little smile too.

They were silent for a moment.

"So does that record ever get like... expunged?" Adam asked, frowning. Was expunged the right word? Wow, he was feeling these beers fast.

Dale sighed wearily. "No. Not really." He shrugged. "And it's not just employers—sooner or later everybody finds out." He rolled his eyes. "I don't get a lot of second dates," he growled with irritation. "Every guy says they want a bad boy, but as soon as they find out you have a record they're gone." He played with his bottle cap in his hands.

Adam stared at him. "Every g-"

No fucking way.

A world of possibilities opened up in Adam's head. Was Dale into him? He was being awfully nice right now for someone who ostensibly hated him. Was all of the awkwardness ... sexual tension? Is that what Kate had wanted to tell him?

After a moment Dale realized what he had said. His eyes widened and he turned beet red.

Adam leaned forward, grinning. "Daaaaale..."

The ranger turned threateningly toward him, his eyes dark and angry. He launched out of his chair. "Okay! Break over!" he snarled. "Back to work. Let's go." He started to walk past Adam, back inside.

"Hey hey heeeey!" Adam said, remaining seated. "Chill, bro! C'mon, man, sit back down." He reached for the ranger, taking Dale by the hand.

Dale froze, staring at him, eyes shocked and accusing.

Adam tightened the grip of his big hand around Dale's hand. He dwarfed Dale's fingers, and he made sure his grip of the ranger's hand was not subtle. Dale's hand was hot in his grasp.

"Hey man, it's cool!" Adam said. He grinned disarmingly. "Relax! I'm bi!"

Dale stared at him. His jaw dropped open. "No way," he said. "That's impossible."

Adam frowned. "Pretty sure it's possible."" He frowned. "Why do gay dudes always say that? Bisexual people do exist, you know. We're not like unicorns or vampires or w... whatever." He tugged on Dale's hand. "Now c'mon, sit back down."

Frowning, Dale edged back into his seat. He still looked like he thought he was being pranked. "Did Katie put you up to this?" he asked, low and dangerous.

Adam frowned. "First of all, if Kate knew you even suggested that she was in on a mean prank like that, she would yell at you for so long it would cause a mass migration."

Dale considered. He believed that. "Okay, point."

Adam cracked a smile. "Secondly... Katie figured me out?"

Dale, deep in thought, pondered. "Yeah, I guess. She's... good with people." He grumbled.

Adam leaned forward. "Aww. That must be why she tolerates your grumpy ass!" he said. "She knows you have a heart of gold, eh?"

Dale glowered at him.

"Anyway, yeah. Relax. I'm cool. We're just two dudes who like dudes."

Dale stared at him. His eyes widened slighly as he looked up.

Adam lowered his voice and spoke a little slower. "Two... smokin' hot dudes who like dudes. Alone. Together. In the middle of the woods." He leaned forward, grinning.

Dale blushed, hard, but he didn't look upset. He had turned red a few times already, but now he flushed deep crimson. To Adam, he looked pretty excited.

"So ahhh, I have some ideas for how to spend your lunch break. And I think you're going to like it more than cheap beer."

Dale frowned, his lips tightly together. He looked nervous. "I don't know, Chaney," he said. "I'm awful partial to those beers."

Adam chuckled. "Oh, yeah? So if I stood up and… walked over there… and climbed right on top of that bench with you, you'd still rather stick to that beer?" he asked, teasingly.

Dale stared at him, processing, and broke eye contact, letting out a shaky breath. "I think you talk too much, Chaney," he said.

Adam stared at him, and then frowned.

Dale swallowed hard. "You really should shut the fuck up, and get over here and actually do something."

Adam stared at him a moment, his brain slowly processing that sentence, and then he silently lifted himself to his feet, grinning. "Yes, sir," he said, stepping forward.

The older man watched him come.

The bench Dale was on had no arms but it did have a back, part of the side railing of the deck. Adam planted his hands on the back rail, on either side of Dale's shoulders, and hoisted himself up onto the bench, on his knees, straddling the ranger and pinning him to the bench. Underneath him, the ranger's legs were muscular and strong, and Adam felt himself stir in his work pants already.

Dale swallowed, staring up at him, and shivered. Adam dwarfed the older man, but he got a feeling Dale was kind of into that. Dale looked nervous but he looked eager, too, staring up at Adam with wide eyes, his mouth slightly open. Adam had pegged the older man a long time ago as someone not good with people, but that was just fine—Adam had no problem taking care of everything.

He leaned in for a kiss, slowly drawing closer to Dale until, just like that, their lips were touching.

There was nothing at first, just contact, like they had bumped accidentally—Dale's open mouth and Adam's closed one. Adam pursed his lips, gently kissing the ranger, and after a moment Dale responded, silently relaxing. Dale leaned forward, too, getting into it, and now they really met, both working their mouths, lips rubbing hard against one another. Adam slipped his tongue into Dale's mouth and the ranger let him, sucking on his tongue, and Adam could feel the ranger's bristly stubble scratching his face.

Adam definitely leaned toward girls but there was something absolutely unbeatable about making out with a dude.

Dale reached up, almost hesitantly, to put his hands on Adam's flanks, and Adam reached up to pull the ranger's cap off, cupping Dale's chin with his other hand, holding his head in place. They fought each other in the kiss, their teeth briefly scraping against one another.

Dale let out a little whimper, and it made Adam's heart pound. The ranger was really getting into it. Adam pushed down, fighting the ranger, pushing his hips forward. He was already hard in his work pants and he pressed his erection against Dale's stomach. Adam wasn't normally this aggressive but he was buzzed and excited and he definitely got the vibe that Dale was into it. He held Dale's head hard, crouched over him, pinning him down against the back of the bench.

Adam broke the kiss and nibbled at Dale's beard. The ranger let out a shuddery breath and squirmed pleasantly underneath him, and now Adam could feel how hard Dale was too. Still holding Dale's chin, he gently tilted the ranger's head back and bit at his neck.

Dale bristled. "Chaney," he whimpered.

It sounded like a good whimper to Adam, so he kept going. It was painful to be hunched over in the weird position so he leaned forward, and bit the side of Dale's neck.

Dale stiffened, and let out a hot little snort. He grunted, arching his back, pushing against Adam's chest. Adam could feel Dale's erection jabbing him in the ass, and he put a little more weight on it, as he bit his way around. He kissed his way back and bit Dale on the neck, hard but not hard enough to hurt, toward the back of his neck.

Dale stiffened again, but this time it was different.

Adam lifted his head, about to ask if that was too much, when suddenly Dale snarled—actually snarled—and threw his entire body weight against Adam's chest.

"Unngh!" Adam grunted, crashing backwards off the bench. He missed cracking his head on the other bench by just a few inches, slamming down on his back on the cold wood. The entire deck thundered and shook under his weight, and both of his empty bottles tipped over with loud clanks and rolled noisily away.

Dale was on his chest in a second. "GET OFF OF ME!" he snarled, from four inches away.

Adam held perfectly still, eyes wide. Stunned, he just stared.

Dale glared at him for a moment, and then blinked in surprise, as if coming out of a trance. He sat up, looking horrified, and covered his mouth with his hands. He was straddling Adam's legs, sitting on Adam's cock, which stubbornly refused to go down. It hurt.

Adam shifted uneasily. "Heeyyyy," Adam said sofly, holding his hands up. "Eaaaasy," he said. "Sorry, man. No more rough play. Whatever you want to do. Sorry about the bites." He swallowed.

Dale stared at him, covering his mouth, eyes wide. Finally he opened his mouth, and his voice was low and shaky. "I'm... I'm sorry. I don't know what... I... ." He couldn't get a sentence out, and he finally slid off of Adam and scrambled to his feet. He turned and strode back toward the doors.

Adam sat up, eyes wide. "Dale?" he asked. "Buddy?" He got clumsily to his feet, thunking on the cold deck. Dale was already long gone.

Adam cautiously picked his way after him, crossing the threshold into the building. He pulled the door shut behind himself, eyes wide. "Hey, whoa, wait!" he called after the ranger. "Dale, what's the matter?" He followed, concerned, but Dale was already all the way accross the station, headed toward the stairs. Adam was sure Dale was going to dart down the stairs and completely ghost him but the ranger made a sharp turn at the sofas near the door.

"I'm gonna lay down. I'm... I'm not right," Dale said, shaking his head. He was still deeply blushing and wouldn't make eye contact. To Adam's eyes, Dale looked as startled by his own behavior as Adam had been.

Adam grit his teeth. "Hey, I'm real sorry about that, man. You can top if you want to. I'm verse, I don't give a shit."

Dale turned to look at him, his face a mask of concern and shame, and shook his head. "You don't want to be with me, Chaney," he said. "I'm a fuckin' mess."

Adam frowned, but after a moment, he couldn't really come up with a response to that.

"Alright, buddy," he finally said. "Come, uh, come get me if you change your mind."

Dale stared at him for a moment, and then sat down, disappearing out of view. A moment later Adam heard one of his heavy boots thunking on the wood floor, and then the other.

Adam stared after him, letting out a long, shaky breath.

After a moment his arm started tingling.

Adam looked down. He had four identical scrape marks running down the length of his left forearm, stopping just above his left wrist. They were fingernail marks, deep enough to hurt and turn bright red. A tiny drop of blood started to well in one of the scratches in the center of his forearm.

He stared. It had been so fast. He hadn't even realized Dale had done it.

Shivering, Adam took a glance at the couch, and then returned to his work.

***

Baffled, Adam tried to remember what he was doing. In a daze, he located his screwdriver and turned back to the gutted section of wall he had been working on.

That had been weird, even by the standards he was coming to apply to Dale. Hope I didn't overstep, he thought. Maybe as an ex-con Dale was a lot more jumpy. Adam frowned. I really should have talked about that more, he thought.

Sighing, Adam figured he had blown his only chance. Maybe he should ask Kate what to do. If he ever talked to any of the rangers ever again.

Maybe I can ask her tomorrow when she shows up at 2:00 pm, since I'm still going to be here trying to get this screw out of this junction box, Adam thought, bitterly. He was half-tempted to just rip out the entire junction box.

And then he stared at the opening in the wall. Wait a minute. He was tearing out the entire junction box. It wasn't to code. The 110-line he had been fighting with was attached to a junction box that he had been planning to replace anyway.

Sticking his head into the hole, he discovered two perfectly intact screwheads staring cheerfully back at him. With them out of the way, the entire box could go in the trash, with the miserable 110-line still attached to it. Why hadn't he seen that earlier?

Shaking his head, Adam took a deep breath. He'd been frustrated and careless earlier. The break, as baffling as it was, had at least cleared his head. He was a little buzzed and a lot less stressed now—he might actually get out of here in a reasonable amount of time after all.

Glancing back at the couch, Adam listened for a moment. Not a sound out of Dale.

Shaking his head, Adam went back to work.

***

2:28 AM

Adam worked fast after that, and an hour and a half later, he finished up. He twisted the last wire just before two-thirty, finishing about an hour earlier than he would have guessed.

The walls looked like hell and there was a lot of cleanup to take care of—the second floor kind of looked like the walls had exploded—but he could stop by in the morning and put in a couple hours on his way to drop off the county truck. Friday was Adam's day off, and he could take his sweet time.

Besides, his thoughts kept drifting back to Dale, and he decided he needed to go somewhere. He still couldn't figure out what had happened and he needed some kind of sleep before he had any hope of cracking the case.

I should at least check on him before I leave, Adam thought. Quietly, Adam walked lightly over to the back of the couch, and just before he cleared it, he noticed a peculiar smell. He paused and sniffed the air, wrinkling his nose.

While working inside mildewy, water-damaged walls, and swimming in his own cloud of evaporated Right Guard, Adam hadn't noticed the peculiar odor the ranger station had taken on. It smelled… musty. It was a bit like wet dog. He cocked his head. Maybe it was the books Dale had been working on. That's weird, he thought.

Adam cleared the back of the couch, and stopped short, sucking in a sharp, startled breath.

Dale was sprawled out on the couch, eyes closed and mouth hanging open, and he was so soaked in his own sweat that his white t-shirt had become transparent. Adam saw a thick patch of black chest hair at the center of Dale's barrel chest, running all the way down the subtle rise of his stomach. His skin was flushed and his face was damp, and his short black hair was matted to his scalp. He took fast, shallow breaths, his mouth hanging open, his eyes closed and his brow gently furrowed. Even in his sleep, he looked upset.

"Holy shit," Adam breathed.

Dale flinched awake and opened his eyes, staring blearily at Adam. "Uggghhh," he groaned. He turned his head slowly to regard Adam. "Who's that?" Dale stared at him a long time, wrinkling his nose and blinking slowly. "Chaney?" he asked, hesitantly.

Adam frowned. He stepped around the couch, completely forgetting their earlier bizarre encounter. Letting out a sigh, he lowered his massive frame into a kneeling position, next to the ailing ranger. "Dale?" he asked, quietly. "Are you okay?"

Dale took a few shallow breaths and stared dazedly back at him. "Damn," he said, quietly. "I guess not." He swallowed and considered for a moment. "I guess this is the flu or something. I feel weak as a kitten. I never felt like this before."

Adam nodded slowly.

Dale squeezed his eyes shut and tried to raise himself to a seating position. He made it up onto his elbows before he groaned and settled down. "Are you heading out?" he asked, his eyes half-closing.

Adam swallowed. "Uh, not yet. I got some cleanup to do first."

Dale half-opened his eyes and squinted at Adam suspiciously. "Thought you were going to do that in the morning," he grunted. His voice sounded like gravel.

"Are you sure you're okay?" Adam asked.

Dale nodded. "I'm fine. Go home," he said, swallowing.

Adam cleared his throat. "Uh, no can do. I gotta be finished by morning," he lied. "Listen, do you want something to drink? How about I open a window for you? You look like you're burning up."

Dale frowned at him, and then turned his head away, grunting. He rolled onto his side, away from Adam, crossing his arms over his chest. "Go home, Adam," he said, his back to him. "I'm not worth it."

Adam considered for a moment, and then reached up with one big hand. It was an impulsive move, probably brought on by the late hour and his sleep deprivation. He reached up and gently took Dale Wallace's hand, holding his thick fingers very gently and resting his own hand over Dale's waist. It wasn't meant to be a provocative gesture, just a comforting one.

The ranger stiffened, and looking longingly over his shoulder. He opened his mouth, took a breath as if to say something, but remained silent. After a moment, he rolled back over with a frustrated sigh.

Adam sighed softly. "Okay, Dale," he said, raising himself to his feet.

Before he did, he squeezed Dale's hand.

The ranger did not visibly react.

Before he got back to work, Adam found a tall glass in the break room. He filled it with cold water and set it on the coffee table behind Dale. The ranger did not visibly stir, and Adam didn't say another word.

***

3:21 AM

Cleanup lasted another forty-five minutes. Adam took his time.

Overnight Shift

When he was coming up on three-thirty in the morning, he decided he couldn't stall any longer and still be remotely coherent tomorrow. His day off was probably completely shot, as he would probably sleep in till noon and somehow still be exhausted and disoriented all day long, but if he stayed awake stalling any longer he would be completely non-functional. He wasn't eighteen anymore.

Carrying a plastic contractor bag around inside the offices, picking up drywall chunks and electrical debris, Adam decided he would sleep in one of the recliners flanking Dale's sofa. One of the other rangers would be in at eight a.m., and they could take over Dale's care at that point. But, until then Adam wasn't going anywhere. Dale looked really bad, and Adam was legitimately worried.

He picked up the last few severed pieces of coiled electrical conduit. The pieces looked like scattered disemboweled intestine, tangled up and strewn about the floor, as if a pack of predators had successfully executed a large kill.

Picking up the last piece, he blinked and stared at it. Wow, he thought. Where did that thought come from? Shaking his head, reflecting on the bizarre nature of sleep deprivation, Adam stepped to the back of the couch.

He gasped.

Dale wasn't on the couch any longer. He had rolled off at some point, and now he was on all fours a few feet away. He had managed to squirm out of both his shirt and his work pants, leaving him clad only in white cotton boxers, a slick sheen of sweat, and wet matted curls of black body hair. Dale's chest was close to the floor with his sweat-soaked muscles bulging from the strain of struggling to hold himself up. Under absolutely any other circumstances it would have been hot as hell, but with conditions as they were Adam felt his stomach turn over in a wave of horror-induced nausea.

He hurried over to the ranger's side and dropped to his knees. "Dale!" he cried. "What's the matter? What are you doing?" Up close, he could see the man was shaking, too, heavy tremors racking the thick muscles of his arms and legs.

34

Dale shook his head, breathing fast and shallow, his teeth clenched and his lips pulled back. He looked like he was in agony. "B-burning up," he grunted. "An' my stomach's doin' something horrible. D-dunno wha's wrong with me."

"Why didn't you ask me for help?!"

Dale shook his head, still trembling. "F-forgot you were here," he said, and then shivered mightily. He dipped his head and squeezed his eyes shut, gasping for breath, and arched his back, hissing in pain.

Adam stared at him, wide-eyed, and set his jaw. "You look really bad, Dale," he said. "I'm taking you to the hospital."

Dale sucked in a breath. "Okay," he gasped, and somehow, the grizzled ranger's immediate consent was the scariest possible response he could have given.

Adam shook his head. "Fucking hell, it's a good thing you're a little guy," he said. He thought for a moment. "Okay. Uh, I'm gonna get you up on the couch, and we're gonna get your pants on. Then I'mma throw you in my truck and we'll drive down to County General, okay?"

Hissing in pain, Dale didn't respond. After a long moment, he grunted out a raspy agreement.

Adam nodded. Holy shit. His heart was pounding. What if he'd gone home for the night?

Leaning forward, he slid both of his big arms under Dale's sweaty chest, one above and the other below the ranger's arm. Dale's skin was hot to the touch, much hotter than it should have been, and clammy, and absolutely dripping with sweat.

He edged Dale toward the sofa, gritting his teeth. Dale gasped in pain, his voice taking on a high-pitch keen to it.

Grimacing, Adam started to lift him up, and Dale suddenly stiffened, crying out in pain. "Aarrrgh!" he roared, snapping both hands up to clamp over his head, and if Adam hadn't been holding him his face would have smashed into the hardwood.

"Dale, what is it?!" he cried.

"Arrrrgh! My head!" Dale cried, writhing in his arms. The ranger squirmed right out of his grasp, crashing over onto his right side. He threw his head back, arched his back, and started thrashing around like a panicked animal, his head inches from the hardwood base of the sofa. One of his flailing feet caught the edge of the coffee table, and the glass Adam had brought him flew off the table and shattered on the floor.

Adam lunged forward and grabbed the ranger's flailing head and thick shoulder. It took all of his weight to hold him in place. "Dale, stop thrashing

You're going to hurt yourself!" He swallowed. "I think I'm gonna call 911," he said, loudly. His hands were starting to shake.

Dale let go of his head with his right hand and shot sideways to grasp Adam's wrist. He held on like a man drowning. "Don't leave me!" he cried, his voice high and desperate.

Adam tried to pull his wrist back, but the ranger's grasp was tight, painfully tight. "I'm not leaving you," he said. "I can't get you down the stairs by myself! I need to call 911! Dale, let go!"

And then something happened.

Adam felt it before he saw it. The palm of Dale's hand, hot and clammy, took on such a… unique tactile sensation that Adam recognized it immediately—despite its utter impossibility, he felt leather. The skin of his wrist, under Dale's palm, told him he was feeling hot, soft, leather.

Forgetting his pain for a moment, forgetting even Dale's apparent agony, Adam looked down.

Dale's fingers were clenching and unclenching, but they were moving in a different way, as well. Even though it was happening right in front of him it took Adam a moment to process that— Dale's fingers were growing thicker. They were growing thicker, right before Adam's eyes. The entire sensation of Dale's hand, clamped onto his wrist became something altogether inhuman, because what was happening to Dale was completely impossible, expanding from within and actually growing in size. It felt more like a blood pressure cuff inflating around him.

He tried to look at the palm of Dale's other hand, but the ranger had it curled into a fist at his side. Insanely, this hand was also bigger.

Dale started jerking suddenly, arching his back and throwing his head back, all the veins and tendons in his neck standing out like steel cables under his skin. His pecs and abs tensed too, the muscles of his arms standing out as rigid and distinctive as an anatomical model.

As Adam watched, Dale's chest hair started to thicken. It was happening on the backs of his arms, too, and then his forearms. Dale was a fairly hairy guy to begin with, covered in vast swatches of coal-black hair, but now there was more growing right as Adam watched. The hair on the back of his hands grew so thick that his skin was no longer visible, like a dense beard... or fur. It looked like fur.

As Adam watched, astonished at the sight, his brain started to do a funny thing. It kind of lost its anchor on reality and gently drifted away, like a balloon, soft and gentle on the breeze. He felt dazed and light-headed.

"Dale?" he asked, his own voice seeming to come from far away.

"Hrrrrnnnnngggghhh!" Dale grunted, through clenched teeth, clamping down on Adam's wrist hard enough to cut off the circulation to his hand. "Hhrrrrrllp me!" he gasped, shaking violently, with... with... whatever was happening now spreading up the rest of his arms. By now Dale had grown so much hair on his clenched, muscular arms that it looked like he'd reached shoulder-deep into an oil drum.

Adam heard cracking and popping noises, like knuckles cracking only much louder, and with a startled gasp he realized that it was like knuckles cracking, except it was all the joints in Dale's body. His actual knuckles cracked, loudly, and then his elbows, and then his shoulders. Crack cr-crack pop CRACK!

The joint-popping followed the seemingly unstoppable tide of thick hair, and Adam noticed, to his astonishment, that in his pained writhing, Dale's muscles appeared to be increasing in size. His shoulders and arms seemed to widen, and not just the muscles, the bones were shifting too, and even under all that hair Adam could tell his biceps were thicker and more rounded. In mere moments, Dale had probably gone up at least two shirt sizes.

Dale arched his back, half-tucking his elbows under his sides, and had thankfully finally let go of Adam's wrist, leaving five deep half-moon-shaped cuts and an already-formed bruise in the shape of a giant hand.

Hair—no, it really did look like thick black fur, thicker than any normal human had grown since the Paleolithic era—now covered Dale's arms and moved in over his pecs, radiating out from the center of his chest at the same time.

The waves of fur broke against one another, the ranger's chest covered in fur like he was wearing a thick sweater, and as they made contact something happened inside his body. Suddenly, the fur erupted out of him, from head to toe, masking his face and covering his stomach, thickening even further on his legs and the tops of his feet. His whole body started to change, too, most notably his legs. His ankles cracked and popped as his feet seemed to break and restructure themselves. There were definitely joints bending the wrong way, and Adam felt a wave of nausea twist his stomach into knots at the sight.

Dale howled in agony and pulled his thick quads in against his chest, trying to curl into a fetal ball. "Earrrrgghhh!" he yowled, letting out a horrible sound like a feral animal's death cry.

At least part of his brain was wondering what the fuck he was doing, but Adam reached for Dale's big hand and clasped it in his own. He held it palm-to-palm, locking their thumbs together, and comfirming that yep, that was definitely a leather pawpad.

Dale Wallace was straight-up turning into a fucking werewolf.

Once Adam had at least tentatively accepted the obvious, his brain helpfully checking out into full-on disassociation, the rest of the transition was much easier to understand. Dale moaned in pain as his face distended, his jaw cracking and popping as he spontaneously grew a muzzle. He made a gagging, choking noise, snapping his new mouth open, and Adam realized he had been choking on his own lupine tongue.

Dale—or the Dale-wolf, Adam supposed—was practically straight out of a monster movie now. He was shivering and shuddering and trembling violently on the floor, and while some part of Adam's brain told him he should be running and screaming by now, he just couldn't bear to leave the ailing ranger. He was the only one here. He couldn't just leave.

Dale jerked violently, thrashing his thick legs in the air, and Adam looked down and saw the back of his boxers bulging and realized what was happening now. Briefly letting go of the ranger's thick hand, he tugged the waistband of his boxers down. As he expected, Dale was growing a thick bushy tail, and as soon as it had room to move he calmed down considerably.

It looks like movie effects, he thought, idly. It did look like state-of-the-art CGI, right in front of his face.

Dale's tail finished growing in, ending up almost two full feet long, and then the wolf just went limp, crashing pathetically onto his side. He lay there, panting desperately, his long, wide tongue lolling out and laying flat on the hardwood. Adam was now on his other side, watching him, silently.

The ranger was now a movie-perfect werewolf. He was thick with muscle, like a fur-covered Olympic weightlifter, and bore claws on each finger as big as the head of a screwdriver. He was all-black, except for a dusty-white patch around his mou-… at the end of his muzzle. His amber-colored eyes were half-closed, and he panted desperately, still shivering violently from time to time.

Swallowing nervously, Adam stared at the prone werewolf.

Holding his breath, he slowly leaned forward on his knees, peering silently over the wolf's frame toward his face.

"ROWRRRRROO!" the wolf howled at him, abruptly thrashing over onto his back.

Adam was so keyed up on adrenaline and so startled that he wasn't even consciously aware of leaping backwards—one second he was kneeling in front of the wolf, and the next he was falling ass-over-teakettle over the back of the couch.

He flailed wildly, his big arms and legs pin-wheeling, and crashed over the short bookcase behind the couch, scattering pamphlets and reference books everywhere. He landed hard on his side in the middle of the floor, slamming his head down on the pine flooring, his arm flat out next to him.

And then, between the shock and the impact, Adam's brain took a little break, and everything went black for awhile.

∗∗∗

When he came to, he could hear growling.

Adam's scrambled thoughts reordered themselves in a hurry. As soon as he felt the wood floor under his head and arms, he remembered where he was. He lifted his head fast, ignoring the way the world spun around like an off-balance top.

Dale Wallace was gone. In his place, tucked in the corner next to the railing and Adam's only way out, was a snarling, angry-looking, fur-covered man... wolf... thing. It had shaggy black fur, yellow eyes, a long, blunt muzzle, pointed ears and a thick, muscular build. It was awkwardly balanced on its hands and thick digitigrades paws, each the size of a softball, tucked under the animal in an obvious preparation for a leap. Adam noticed, crazily, that the wolf was still wearing Dale's white boxers.

The wolf-beast glared at him, growling. They made eye contact, and Adam quickly came to the conclusion that the thinking, rational, and (most importantly) non-homicidal portion of Dale's brain was now completely absent from this picture. It might as well have been an actual wolf with him in the Nature Center, except that a genuine wolf probably would not have been quite so pissed off. The wolf's ears were tilted back and he was baring his teeth.

Dale was gone. This was an animal now. It was going to attack.

The wolf-beast's thick legs tensed. He leapt.

"Gah!" Adam kicked backward, hard, the heels of his boots scrabbling for purchase on the floor. He flailed backward trying to escape, realized he wasn't going to make it, and lifted his feet up at the last second.

The wolf crashed upon him, crushing his legs against his chest, and suddenly all the air left Adam's lungs in one quick whoosh. The beast sank his teeth into Adam's left boot, and it was like his foot was caught in a vice grip. "Aaaagghh!" he cried, straightening his other leg hard on instinct and panic.

His right boot was planted in the center of the wolf's chest, out of luck more than anything else, and the snarling animal flew backward, slamming against the exterior wall. He collapsed into a seething mass of fur and teeth, tearing down the miniblinds in the process, which dropped out of the window frame like a stage curtain dropping.

Overnight Shift

He still had Adam's left boot in his mouth. Adam wore his boots unlaced, and now one of them was gone.

His heart pounding, Adam kicked back, trying to scramble to his feet.

The wolf dropped his boot and lunged forward, thick claws scrabbling on the hardwood, and leapt at him again. His arc was different this time, longer, and Adam realized with blood-curdling terror that the animal had planned to overshoot and miss his dangerous feet—the wolf was adapting. Adam quickly yanked his arms and legs in over his torso because now the fucking thing was going to land right on his ch-

The black beast slammed directly down on top of him, his snapping jaws inches away from Adam's face.

"Get off!" Adam screamed in horror, as he shoved upward as hard as he could, before the wolf had even stopped moving from the leap.

Adam's already-considerable strength, now fueled by pure fear, lifted the wolf halfway to the ceiling. Carried by his own momentum, the wolf hurtled across the room, a flailing mass of fur and limbs. He crashed onto one of the card tables against the wall of the conference room, smashing it like a cardboard box. The wolf crashed to the floor with two old CRT-monitors and a bank of equipment, with a noise like a dump truck emptying a load of scrap metal. The items on top of the desk shot away like shrapnel, flying off to all corners of the room.

Get up! Get up! Get up! Adam scrambled back onto his feet behind the long sofa, desperate to get off the floor before the wolf's next attack. The animal was surprisingly fast, impossibly fast.

Adam was next to the stairwell, but he didn't have his truck keys, and he genuinely did not think he would make it all the way down the stairs before the wolf caught him. The wolf would drop on top of him like a hawk onto a rabbit before he made it halfway down the stairs.

He bolted for the kitchenette in the opposite corner, which at least had a door he could slam. He thundered across the pine floors, making the entire building shake, stomping across the small station with one boot missing. THUD pffft THUD pffft THUD pffft!

By the time he got halfway there he could hear the wolf right behind him. The animal's claws skittered on the hardwood in a way that made Adam think of a dog's claws on a vet's tile floor, even as a sharp spike of panic shot up his spine.

He made it to the tiny kitchen, barely the size of a jail cell, a split-second before the wolf did. Whirling on his still-booted foot, he threw his entire body weight into hurling the door shut.

The dark-stained wood was preposterously light and made an unsatisfying thunk! sound, and with bone-chilling horror, Adam realized it was a hollow-core door. It was just two thin pieces of wood veneer with maybe a block of Styrofoam between them. It wouldn't stop a German Shepherd, let alone a fully-grown werewolf.

Half a second later, the wolf crashed into the door from the other side. The door bulged at the center, crunching with the unmistakable sound of wood splintering. CRUNNGGHH!

"Awkk!" Adam cried, involuntarily. The door had probably only bought him ten or twenty seconds before the werewolf smashed it to splinters.

He whirled. His only escape was a tiny window he would never fit through, and then he would just be outside with no car keys and no cover. He needed something else. There had to be a knife in the kitchen, right?!

Adam lunged for the nearest drawer.

CRUNNGGH! went the door again, a loud, wet crunching. The wolf yowled in frustration from the other side of the door. He clawed viciously at it, like a cat, his claws scrabbling violently on the wood.

In the third drawer, he found a huge chef's knife. He held it in his hands, grimacing. The blade was ten inches long and razor sharp. It could have been a prop in a horror movie.

Adam stared at it, his big hands shaking.

A knife. Was he really considering this? Was he really going to use a fucking chef's knife to stab Ranger Dale? The guy who organized nature books for seven-year-olds and, by Adam's own reasoning, was probably just a cripplingly shy and lonely old man?

He swallowed hard. Silently, he shook his head.

CRUNNGGHH-CRACCKKKTH!

Adam jerked in shock, dropping the knife with a clatter into the sink, knowing what he would see in the half-second before he saw it. The door had a huge crack down the middle, light shining through from the main room. He couldn't see the wolf, but something struck him as important about the crack itself.

It was probably only five feet above the floor. He had to look down at it.

The wolf was not small, but he was smaller than Adam.

Small enough to beat?

CRUNNGGHH! went the door as the wolf slammed into it, and the flimsy wood bulged inward exactly where Adam thought it would, right were Dale's shoulder would have been. His height hadn't changed much. Adam would still tower over him.

He stared, wide-eyed. Could he really do this? Could he… could he take the wolf?

The door was shot. One more hit would take it out.

Adam took a step back, planted his booted foot on the linoleum, and blasted forward, charging the damaged door with the intent to go straight through it.

Adam hit the door and annihilated it, crashing through it like it hadn't even been there. The hollow-core door shattered like tissue paper, splitting with a sharp CRACK! down the middle and bursting away from him on either side, tiny bits of wood shrapnel and sawdust exploding in all directions. It was a terrific impact, one that jammed his shoulder hard into the socket and jarred him through his entire skeletal system, but it did not slow Adam down. He was still at full speed when he crashed into the werewolf, who had been about to hit the door from the other side.

Hitting the werewolf was exactly like one of the brain-jarring impacts Adam remembered from high school football, except this time he wasn't wearing his padding or a helmet. It was like doing a belly-flop off the high-dive, if someone had drained the pool ahead of time. As the one with greater mass, however, Adam also had greater momentum, and literally lifted the werewolf off his paws.

They were falling, suddenly, and Adam just let it happen. He grabbed the wolf's arms—God, he's solid muscle!—as they plummeted toward the floor, and as the hardwood rocketed up toward them he held the animal firmly in front of him.

The wolf landed on his side, and grunted as he hit the ground, but when Adam's entire crushing body weight landed on top of him he let out a sharp, agonized yelp as the air left his body. He jerked, violently, teeth clenched, writhing in shock and gasping for air, struggling on his side under Adam's weight.

The animal regained his wits almost immediately, faster than Adam, and he rolled onto his stomach and tried to squirm away.

"Oh, no you don't," Adam grunted, lunging for the animal. He was on the wolf in an instant, wrapping one thick bicep around the werewolf's throat, climbing on top of him like a wrestler in the wrong weight class. Adam had been on the wrestling team, for about half a semester, and he knew a thing or two about sleeper holds. They were illegal, for obvious reasons, but Adam still knew how to do them. The other boys on the team had traded the knowledge like contraband.

Adam clamped his eighteen-inch bicep around the wolf's throat, cutting off both the flow of air to his lungs, and blood to his brain. "Dale, if you're in there, just go quietly," he grunted. He pinned the wolf's thick arms with his other arm, squeezing him as tightly as he could. If he had done this to human Dale, the man would have screamed in pain, if he could still breathe.

The wolf stiffened and snarled as best as he could with no airflow—the beast was terrifying, all muscle and anger—but Dale had been, what, 5'8"? One-eighty, if that? The wolf was no match for Adam, even with teeth and claws. Adam was going to knock him out, restrain him, and then figure out what the fuck to do next.

The wolf that had once been Dale stiffened mightily, and then struggled in earnest. He tried to pull his head out of Adam's grasp, desperately trying to thrash his way out, jerking and slamming against Adam like a hooked shark. Adam felt the moment the wolf stopped fighting out of anger and instead started fighting out of pure panic, in the way that only an animal can, out of fear that Adam was going to gut him and eat him. The animal thrashed violently, crashing up against Adam's stomach hard enough to bruise him, lifting them both up off the ground to slam back down hard enough to shake the building.

"Calm down, God dammit!" Adam snapped, squeezing as hard as he could, and the wolf writhed in pain and panic.

It was a perfectly-executed sleeper hold, and in ten seconds flat, the wolf's entire thick body went limp. He twitched a few times, and that was it.

Adam held him another few seconds to be sure, struggling to hold up the heavy animal, and then relaxed.

The werewolf dropped limply to the floor. Adam collapsed on top of him, panting desperately.

Shuddering, he let out a shaky breath.

***

The wolf was only out for half a minute, but it was enough time for Adam. By the time the animal even began to stir, Adam had already laid him out face-up between the couch and the coffee table and lashed the animal's wrists together—in front of him—with heavy insulated wire. He had also tied his muzzle shut, but that had been just a couple feet of wire looped around the base of his muzzle and wrapped around the back of his head. Adam wasn't sure that would even prevent him from opening his mouth.

That was about all he had time for, though. He had barely sunk down to the floor, still breathing hard, when the werewolf's golden eyes fluttered open.

He stared blankly at Adam, seemingly confused, and then his eyes widened. He tugged on his bonds, squirmed in place, and then looked fearfully up at Adam, eyes wide and alarmed.

Adam frowned down at him. "Yeah," he said. "That's how that went. I kicked your furry ass!" It was a stupid thing to say, but Adam was still filled with adrenaline.

The wolf took one look at him and began thrashing.

Adam gasped. "Oh, shit! No, it's okay!" he cried, lunging toward Dale.

The wolf yanked at his bonds, making a panicked high-pitched yelp. He yanked at his bonds, and Adam could see the wires tightening. The animal was going to rip off his own skin if Adam didn't stop him.

"Hey, hey, hey!" Adam yelled. He lunged for the wolf and sank his fingers deep into the animal's scruff. He tightened his grasp, pulling up the wolf's scruff until his skin was taut and his head tilted backward. Adam had owned several big dogs growing up, and briefly been a vet tech, and the maneuver felt practiced, like riding a bike. He held down the wolf's paws with his other hand, just able to get his big human hand around both of Dale's furry wrists.

The wolf stared up at him with panicked, wide eyes, a thick white ring visible around his golden irises, and he stopped struggling almost immediately. He flopped over onto his back, staring up at the human, half-opening his muzzle and panting.

"That's it," Adam cooed. "It's okay, buddy. We're done. I kicked your ass to show my dominance, now we're done. I'm not gonna hurt you. Shhhhhhh."

The wolf stared up at him with ears folded back, and terror in his eyes.

Adam let out a long sigh. "I didn't even want to do that, you know," he told him. "You attacked me." He frowned. "If you just chill out I won't have to defend myself." He let out a shaky breath. "I guess we know why you lost your shit earlier. You were starting to wolf out."

Staring up at him, the wolf swallowed.

Adam let out a shaky breath. Slowly, experimentally, he released his death-grip on the wolf's scruff.

The wolf just stared up at him, eyes wide and blank.

Adam stared at him. "Dale," he whispered. "Are you in there at all?" He stared at the wolf in his arms.

There was no response.

Letting out another sigh, Adam let the wolf slide out of his lap. He laid the big animal on the ground and scooted a few feet away, sitting on his ass against the side of the askew loveseat, his big feet—one still booted, one in just the sock—out between him and the wolf.

They stared at each other. The wolf remained silent, breathing softly. He was arguably calmer than Adam himself, whose heart was still pounding in his chest, with his body covered in scratches and sawdust.

After a moment, the wolf silently looked away. His eyes were less wide, but he had a very expressive muzzle, and he still clearly looked a little wary. He looked like a big dog at the vet, to be perfectly honest.

Adam took a good look at the werewolf for the first time.

He frowned.

The wolf was… kind of hot.

Oh my God, what is the matter with me, Adam thought, putting his head in his hands. But, when he looked up, the laid-out wolf was still the same solid mass of muscle.

And why not? Dale had been hot. He was a short-stacked blue-collar daddy. Now, the wolf had the same short-stack frame, except he was thick as hell. He was still overwhelmingly human-shaped. If Dale had gone on a gym binge for a few solid months, and put on a wolf mask, this is what he would look like. Well, if he'd also been wearing digitigrade leg prosthetics. With eight-inch-wide wolf paws.

Frowning, Adam looked over the mostly-naked werewolf, and this time he let himself really look. The animal had Dale's thick shoulders and narrow waist, but with a lot more muscle packed on. The wolf's pecs were like slabs of meat, and he had a neatly-laid grid of cobblestone abs visible even under his soft fur. And the werewolf had a solidly fat package in his—Dale's—boxers. Weirdly, Adam found himself wondering about the exact layout.

Adam frowned. He hadn't quite un-horned himself from his earlier encounter with Dale, and now it was coming back. Adam had always found movie werewolves kind of hot. Surely, this was just carryover horniness. Right?

Adam looked at the wolf's face, and caught the animal glancing furtively back at him. As soon as he made eye contact, the animal snapped his eyes away, his ears tilting back like he'd been caught digging through the trash. It was classic submissive behavior.

Adam stared at him, and suddenly his jaw dropped open. "Oh, my GOD," he said. "Am I your alpha now? Because I beat you?" He considered. Was that even a real thing? He had read somewhere that the whole idea of an 'alpha' was a myth but he had barely been paying attention.

The wolf said nothing, holding perfectly still on his side, his gaze averted under Adam's eyes. As Adam watched, the animal lifted his bound wrists, exposing his stomach.

Adam stared at him, his mouth hanging open. "Can you… understand me?" he whispered.

No response.

Is that Dale in there? he wondered. Or was it just a dumb animal? Could it be both?

Would this wolf's submissiveness carry over to Dale, when he changed back? If he changed back? Was the wolf's submissiveness because of Dale in the first place?

Lifting himself to his knees, moving slowly, just to see what would happen, Adam leaned over and reached down, and gently reached toward the wolf's stomach with his thick fingers.

The wolf that had been Dale didn't growl, or snap, or turn his head with foam dripping from his jaws.

Instead, he arched his back gently, lifting his vulnerable belly up toward Adam's hand, and let out a soft snort.

Adam touched the wolf's stomach. He was surprisingly warm. And his reaction was even more surprising—the wolf let out a soft, shuddering breath.

He wasn't scared anymore. He… seemed to like it.

Swallowing hard, Adam pulled his hand back. Shaking his head, he stood up from the pine floor.

Puzzled, the wolf looked up and watched him.

Adam shook his head. He had an incredibly strong impulse to dig his fingers into the werewolf's fur and hold him.

It was probably just stress, and sleep deprivation, and hormones. That had to be all it was.

It had to be.

***

"Hi, Kate, it's Adam again. Look, I know this is like the tenth time I've called you in twenty minutes, and I realize you aren't like avoiding me, but I seriously need to get in touch with you because this situation, uh, it is not getting any better and I could really use your help. You said you'd be at a party all night so I'm hoping you're still there." He inhaled. "So, uh, call the station. Thanks. Bye."

The big electrician paced in a circle, one boot still on and one off. Crazily, he hadn't been able to find his second boot. He was scratched all to hell and the bruises Dale and the door had left on him were starting to throb.

After hanging up the phone and turning away from the work area, Adam turned back toward the couch.

The muscular black wolf was crawling around from the side of the couch, hands still bound, moving on all fours. Adam's heart leapt up into his chest and he let out a little screech. The black wolf looked like a ghost straight out of a Japanese horror movie.

"HEY!" he barked, pointing at the air like he was yelling at a German Shepherd.

The wolf flinched, eyes wide and alarmed, and raised his head, his ears folded back. Pushing against the ground with his thick arms, he lifted himself nimbly into a kneeling position. He knelt, his wrists bound before him and his muzzle tied shut, like a prisoner of war.

"Quit moving around!" Adam growled, feeling the hairs on the back of his neck stand up. "Kate's going to call back any minute and then we'll get you... some help." He frowned. "Of some kind... and quit trying to stand up or I'll-"

"Kaaaaaaaaaaayy reeeeeeeeey!" the wolf said.

His jaw dropping, Adam stared at him.

The wolf frowned in concentration, his brow furrowing elaborately, and opened his mouth, playing with his flat, wide tongue. The wire muzzle had been useless after all.

The wolf licked his teeth, his ears flopping around in all directions, and finally looked up at Adam again.

"Kaaaay-dey," the wolf growled, much more clearly. His voice was deep and gravelly, like a long, drawn-out growl.

"Holy shit," Adam responded. He slowly approached the kneeling wolf.

The black animal remained in a kneeling position, staring up at him, but now there was something different about him. Adam looked into his eyes, and as the wolf looked back, he distinctly saw human intelligence. His eyes were golden now, not brown, but he had the same somber, piercing gaze that Dale had worn, and now, for the first time, he really looked like a werewolf version of the ranger.

"Dale?" Adam whispered. "Is that you in there, buddy?" He stepped a few feet closer.

The wolf stared blankly up at him, and for a moment Adam was sure he'd imagined the brief glimpse of the ranger, but then the animal looked down, his ears folding back in thought.

After a moment, taking a long, deep breath, the wolf nodded. "Daaare," he said, swallowing. "I Daaare." The wolf couldn't form the letter "L." Apparently, the Scooby-Doo people were right all along.

"Wow," he said.

The wolf stared at him expectantly. It was a very dog-like stare, but it was a very Dale-like stare, too. For the last four weeks, Dale had watched him with that same expectant gaze. Waiting to see what he would do. It was exactly the same sort of look, but Adam just hadn't made the connection until now.

Adam cocked his head. "Are you… all right?" He didn't know what else to say. This was too weird. It was almost weirder than the transformation itself.

The wolf processed the question, thinking hard about the answer. "Yesss," he growl-hissed. He nodded, too, which looked bizarre and otherworldly to see an animal do, even if he was only half-animal.

Adam swallowed anxiously. "Do you know who I am?"

The big black wolf stared at him for a short time, and then cocked his head. "You… Arram," he said. "You… strong."

Adam furrowed his brow. "What?"

51

The wolf nodded, tilting his ears back. "Strong. Fight." He lifted his bound paws, staring at him. Tilting his muzzle downward, he looked up. "Dare... Dare sub... submit." It was a lot of trouble for him to get the words out, so it must have been important for him to say.

Adam stared at him in disbelief. "What did you say?" he whispered.

The wolf risked a glance up at him, his ears still flat against his head. "Strong. Daare s... ssubmit," he rumbled. He lifted his bound paws by way of explanation, lowering his muzzle and breathing softly.

Adam was struck again by how much the wolf looked like a prisoner, and he abruptly realized that Dale hadn't been attempting to stand. He had lifted himself to his knees intentionally. It was to show Adam he wasn't a threat. He had done it to show his submission.

Something weird happened inside Adam's brain. He felt his conscious mind drift away again, and this time something different took over.

The electrician cocked his head. "Is that so?" he asked, softly.

The black wolf held perfectly still.

Adam took a few steps forward, his remaining boot and his sock making soft, deliberate footfalls on the hardwood. He stopped in front of him.

"Lift your chin then," he said, his own voice sounding half an octave lower. It sounded like it was coming from someone else.

Obediently, without hesitation, the thick werewolf lifted his blunt muzzle, exposing his furry throat. Adam looked him over. The animal looked calm and relaxed. If anything, he seemed to be relieved. It made sense—Dale the wolf was apparently having a really hard time putting thoughts together. He was in no shape to make decisions now, and he knew it. He was vulnerable. He needed help. He needed an alpha wolf figure to get him through this.

Adam thought about it for a minute. This would actually make things a lot easier. If Dale was submissive and pliable, he would be easier to manage until Kate could be reached. Adam wouldn't have to worry about the wolf trying anything if Dale was completely under his control. He and the wolf could just hang out until Kate showed up and doubtlessly came up with a plan to fix all this. The wolf probably knew it too—Adam had already beat him. So, why not submit and benefit from the stronger party's better skills?

He thought about that again. Completely under his control.

Reaching gently forward, Adam brushed the wolf's exposed throat with his thick fingers.

The wolf swallowed reflexively, and shivered, but otherwise did not move. He simply stared complacently at the ceiling, a submissive tower of muscle and fur.

For all intents and purposes, he appeared to be completely passive.

Adam felt like he should really test that, however. Just to make absolutely certain that Dale would be… safe.

"Dale, are you submitting completely to me?" he asked, softly.

The wolf took a moment to process. "Yess," he whispered, holding perfectly still.

"Good. You won't mind proving it, then," he muttered.

Adam lowered himself to his own knees, slowly letting his fingers trail down the front of the wolf's chest. That was a hot button for dogs, wasn't it? They only let you touch their tummy if they were acknowledging that you were the boss.

The wolf shivered, looking up toward the ceiling. He puffed his chest out, exhaling shakily, and Adam saw his thick arms tense up. He watched as the muscles thickened, like steel cables under an inch of soft fur. His wrists were still tied and he tugged gently on the cables binding them.

He trailed his fingers down over the top of the wolf's stomach, between his bound forearms, and the animal let out a soft whimper.

"It's okay," Adam cooed, quietly. "I'm not gonna hurt you." He cocked his head. "I'm not even mad that you tried to fight me." He trailed his thick fingers over the wolf's oversized paws, making contact again just over the waistband of the wolf's boxers. "Don't worry, I'm gonna take good care of you."

Still pointing his muzzle skyward, the wolf nodded awkwardly. He let out a long shaky breath, but he made no effort to squirm away. In fact, his long muzzle had an air of determination, as if he was hell-bent on proving to the bigger man just how complete his submission was.

Adam decided to give him the perfect chance to do that.

Reaching in with both hands, Adam gripped the leg holes of the wolf's boxers and tugged them downward. He did it slowly and deliberately, letting the wolf feel himself be exposed.

Adam had wondered if a wolf's natural state of nudity would carry over to a werewolf, but apparently it was Dale's human modesty that had the most influence on his werewolf form. As his boxers slowly rode down his hips and finally cleared his genitals, the wolf let out a soft whimper. He started panting, fast and shallow.

The wolf wouldn't look down but Adam did. Dale had low-hanging balls covered in fuzzy black fur, almost like velvet, and a plump little skin thing… what was it called? A sheath, he recalled. A fuzzy sheath made up of loose skin covered in fluffy, short black fur. It was fat and full and pointed upwards.

The wolf whined softly and let out a soft, shivery breath, his thick chest heaving as he strained to hold still.

Adam watched him. "Are you feeling nervous, Dale?" he asked. "Do you want me to stop?"

The wolf whined louder now, lowering his muzzle to make eye contact. "No! No stop!" he growled loudly, and then he realized he was staring Adam in the eyes and looked away, his ears folding flat against his head.

"That's so nice to hear," Adam said, wrapping his thick fingers around the wolf's fuzzy ballsack. Dale's balls were surprisingly hot and quite heavy. Adam rolled them in his fingers.

Dale shivered violently and let out a panting gasp, arching his back and gritting his teeth. He raised his bound paws and put them on Adam's left shoulder, staring at him with wide, surprised eyes.

Adam grinned at him from inches away. "You're doing so good, Dale," he said. "I know you're doing this just to please me. I appreciate it." He rolled the werewolf's fat sac in his hand, rubbing the space just under Dale's sheath with the pad of his thick thumb.

Dale squirmed in place, amber eyes wide, but he did not attempt to writhe away. He just knelt there, breathing hard, bracing himself on Adam's thick shoulder, allowing himself to be manhandled. He had submitted, utterly and completely. His expression changed, and Adam knew the wolf was enjoying it.

"That's a good boy, Dale," Adam rumbled. "An hour ago you tried to eat me, and now you're kneeling here with your balls in my hand," Adam gloated. "How does that feel?" His heart was pounding—it felt good to finally show Dale who was boss. He squeezed the wolf's balls gently and tugged on them, probing at the wolf's sheath with his thumb, harder this time. His sheath was hard and full now, and Dale know the wolf's cock would be making an appearance any moment.

Dale stared at him a second longer, and as he stared into Adam's eyes, his own amber eyes began to slide closed.

Adam cocked his head. "Hmm, is that starting to feel good?" He raised his other hand and wrapped his thick fingers around the back of Dale's neck. He rubbed him there, firmly, while he played gently with the wolf's package, and then the wolf's cock began to breach the end of his sheath and telescope slowly outward. Adam moved his hand up and began idly massaging the monster's meat, and the wolf's cock stiffened in his hands. It was hot, and it looked mostly like a human cock, except for a narrower head and a deep red, almost black color.

Dale stared right at Adam, transfixed, and his mouth opened gently. He just looked like a dumb dog, stupid and happy to be getting attention.

Adam could smell him now, too—a deep woodsy musky smell. The wolf was loving this. He was becoming even more submissive. It was perfect. Some part of Adam's brain was aware that he was slowly masturbating a supernatural monster, but everything he forced on Dale made the werewolf more compliant, and he wanted him as pliable as putty. The more secure Adam's role as alpha was, the more he could keep the weaker werewolf in check.

Adam released the wolf's balls and reached up to drag his fingernails through the wolf's stomach fur. Dale's eyes stayed half-closed but his eyebrows arched up, and he let out a soft moist breath and tensed his thick stomach muscles.

"There you go... just relax, bud," Adam rumbled. He dug his fingers into the wolf's ruff and held him hard, rubbing him vigorously all over his thick chest and stomach, his shoulders and his neck, and finally his muzzle. The wolf tensed his muscles and writhed under his hand, and boy, did he feel good to touch. He was such a strong, powerful wolf, even if he was a hell of a lot weaker than Adam.

The wolf was clearly enjoying the sensation just as much. He rumbled softly with his muzzle still half-open, and as Adam watched, a thin trickle of werewolf drool hooked over his thick black lips and trailed off onto his furry chest.

Adam reached up and gently brushed it away with his wrist. He grazed the wolf's muzzle, and something made him hold his hand there. He felt a strange urge to wrap his thick fingers around Dale's muzzle, and so he did.

The wolf closed his eyes completely and arched his back, shivering blissfully. He made a little moaning sound inside his muzzle, and Adam could practically taste his excitement. He felt wild and powerful. Dale would be eating out of his hand in another ten minutes. Literally, if Adam so desired.

He leaned forward, towering intimidatingly over the wolf, staring straight down at him, close enough to ruffle the wolf's short muzzle-fur with his own breath. Still holding the ranger's scruff, Adam let his big hand slide down between Dale's pecs and over his stomach again. He rested his fingers momentarily on the cables still binding Dale's wrists, tugging on them to remind the wolf how helpless he was.

Dale half-opened his eyes, locked on Adam's gaze just inches away, and stared dully into his eyes, transfixed.

Dominate him, something whispered in Adam's mind. Make him yours.

Adam frowned. There was something wrong about this. Face-to-face wasn't the way to truly show a lesser wolf his place, was it? He should be behind him. It was called doggie-style for a reason, wasn't it?

Dale widened his eyes, confused, but by the time he'd furrowed his brow in consternation Adam had already shuffled around behind him. He put one arm around the wolf's waist and the other around his throat, squeezed the wolf tightly against his chest, and shivered violently at the feeling of shaggy fur and rough muscle on his bare arms.

There, that was better. The wolf smelled like the forest in autumn, and Adam was surprised to find his own cock rock-hard and throbbing in his jeans. He hadn't even noticed how erect he'd become until he ground his cock against the thick muscles under Dale's tail. The wolf had such power, but Adam owned all of it.

In front of him, Dale squirmed in place and growled softly, but something in the sound let Adam know it was not a threatening growl. It was a growl of pleasure. He knew that because... because...

Frowning, Adam cocked his head. How in the fuck did he know that-

Abruptly, the Dale wolf let out an impatient growl, probably because Adam had stopped moving. He angled his head around and clacked his teeth together, snapping his jaw shut inches from Adam's face.

What?! Something hot and angry welled up inside Adam. He tightened his big arm around the insolent animal's throat, lunged forward, and snapped his own teeth shut on the top of the wolf's muzzle. He bit him, only for a moment, but hard enough to break skin. He tasted fur and sweat in his mouth.

Dale yelped explosively and flinched, tensing his entire thick body, but he was no match for Adam's superior physicality. He held his tension only for a moment, and then he went completely limp in his arms. If Adam had not been holding him, he would have collapsed to the floor.

Wide-eyed, tasting fur and blood on his teeth, Adam stared in wide-eyed astonishment. He had just bit Dale. What in the holy fuck was that?

Dale craned around to look at him again, but this time his eyes were averted. His ears were tilted back, and his throat was exposed, and he whined submissively like the little pup he might as well have been. He stuck his tongue out, splaying his ears to the side to show there were no hard feelings.

Adam felt himself begin to calm immediately. It was all right. He'd asserted his dominance. The disrespectful pup had been shown his place. He was ready to behave now. He was ready for Adam to own him. He set his jaw and again leaned forward, pressing himself up against Dale's back. The wolf was as good as his property, and when he turned back into a human, he still would be. Opening his mouth, Adam brushed his teeth against the wolf's neck and prepared to bite down.

"HEY I HEARD YOU WERE A WILD ONE! OOOH-WOOO OOOOO OOOOOOOOOOOO!"

A song rang out as loud as a concert speaker, shattering the silence of the ranger station. Both Adam and the wolf flinched hard enough to crash over in opposite directions.

"IF I TOOK YOU HOME IT'D BE A HOME RUN! SHOW ME HOWWW YOU'LL DOOOOO!!"

They both looked wildly about. The wolf was so startled it was almost comical. He looked like a dog when his owner switches on the vacuum.

Cellphone. It was his cellphone. Adam looked around, twisting his head in all directions, trying to locate the phone.

The phone was right there on the coffee table. He'd left it right next to them.

Eyes wide and heart pounding, Adam looked back at the werewolf. Some of the haze cleared in his mind, and he felt like he was waking up from a deep sleep.

Guilty and scared, Dale lowered his head and looked submissively back at him. Swallowing, the wolf awkwardly tugged his boxers back up over his flagging erection. He was so awkward with his hands he could barely grip the elastic. He pawed at it like a domestic dog.

Swallowing, Adam picked up his phone and hit the ACCEPT CALL button. He noticed the clock for the first time. It said 4:24 A.M.

"Hello?" he asked, feeling guilty. What the hell had been happening just now?

"Adam?!" Kate demanded, on the other end of the line. Adam could hear thumping bass from music in the background. "Are you okay?! What's happening?!"

He tried to clear his throat, his mouth full of saliva for some reason. "Kate," he grunted. "Hi. How's it going?" he said, flatly. His head was spinning. He had to concentrate.

"Are you hurt? Is Dale hurt?"

Adam swallowed. Get it together, he told himself. "Uh. Not exactly. He's, not quite himself right now." He stared at the shaggy werewolf. Dale's ears were both perked toward him, and Adam could tell he was listening to both sides of the conversation. The look in Dale's amber eyes did not betray whether or not he understood a single word of it, however.

"Is it that flu he had earlier? Does he need to go to a hospital?"

Adam processed that. "Uh, not really, no. I don't think this is a hospital sort of problem." He considered for a moment. "Maybe a vet."

"What?"

He coughed. "Uh, nevermind. Listen, it would be a lot easier to have this conversation in person. Can you come to the station? Like, as fast as you can possibly get here?"

There was a pause. "Did you guys get into a fistfight or something? Because there was this drywall guy and they ended up-"

Adam let out a sigh. "No, he's just... he's changed." He sighed. "Really, this conversation is totally impossible to have over the phone." He looked back at Dale. The wolf cocked his head innocently.

"Can I talk to him?"

Adam sighed again. "No, I'm afraid you can't."

There was a long pause. "Do I need to call the police?"

Adam gasped. "Jesus Christ, don't do that. We'll never see Dale again. I can't tell you what's happening, but please trust me if you show up with the authorities it's all over for him."

Kate sighed loudly. "My God. All right. I'm on my way. I'm at a party in Elizabethtown, so it's going to take me probably two hours to get back, maybe more. But I'll come right there."

Adam sighed gratefully. "Thank you. Thank God."

There was a short pause. "And listen here—I don't know what's going on, but... if you harm one hair on his head I know about a hundred spots out in those woods where they won't find your corpse until there's nothing left but bones."

Adam felt the hair on his arms bristle at her tone, and he slowly realized that she was deadly serious. "I believe you," he said, and he meant it. "I won't harm a hair on his…" He swallowed, looking back at the wolf. "On his anywhere."

"Mmm-hmmm." There was another short pause. "You're lucky I trust you, Adam."

He let out a breath. "Dude, you have no idea. Just get here quick, okay?"

"Right," she said, and then the line went dead.

He checked the time on his phone. 4:27 A.M. She would make it by 7.

This was shaping up to be a hell of a night.

***

Frowning, Adam turned back to the wolf.

The Dale-wolf had raised himself onto his knees and haunches when Adam returned. He cocked his head as the big electrician approached, and hunched his shoulders, folding his ears back submissively. The black wolf angled his muzzle, staring at Adam expectantly.

Adam felt the hairs on his arms stand up as he watched Dale.

Something had happened to him. Something very strange. Weird and inexplicable feelings had been coming over him.

No, he thought. Might as well say it. Instincts.

He swallowed.

Dale watched him, and now he looked up, wide-eyed.

Adam realized he hadn't said anything. "Uh," he said, clearing his throat. "Kate is on her way. She'll… she'll help us figure this whole thing out." He nodded.

Dale nodded, his big eyes calm and understanding. "Kayyyy-deyyyyy," he rumbled.

Adam nodded. "Yup. Kayy-deyy." He eyed the wolf up and down, warily.

The wolf stared back at him. He cocked his head, confused.

Adam frowned. He didn't want to get too close. Something was happening to him and it seemed to be worse when he got closer to Dale. Idly, he rubbed his scratched-up arms.

Suddenly, Dale moved toward him. It wasn't a threatening move, or even a particularly significant one—all he did was lean forward onto his hands. But Adam wasn't expecting it, and he jerked in shock. "Aah!" he gasped.

Shocked, Dale snapped his head back, his ears folding back against his head. He stared at Adam, startled, and after a moment he began slowly backing away.

Adam let out a shaky breath. He needed to get ahold of himself.

Dale edged away, his ears folded back against his head. He looked freaked out. "A-angry?" he said, softly, hunching his shoulders.

Adam frowned. "No, buddy. I'm just… I just need to think." Adam was feeling claustrophobic. It was hard to concentrate with the wolf's piercing eyes on him. "I think… I think I just need a minute." He swallowed. "I just need a minute alone."

The wolf's eyes widened at the last word. "A… alone?" he whispered. "Aram l-leave?" he asked. He sounded like his grasp of spoken language was eroding. He dipped his muzzle, his pointy black ears splaying in opposite directions. He looked miserable.

Adam grit his teeth. He wanted to run to the wolf and sweep him into his arms. Dale was Adam's charge and look what he was doing to him. But Adam still didn't know what was happening to him. He stared at the wolf, his heart aching, but his mind screamed at him to run. He could hear his blood rushing in his ears.

"You know what?" Adam gasped. "I'm gonna go outside for a minute. I need to go outside and think." He looked around and snatched his truck keys off his toolbox. "I just need to go outside and think, Dale. I'll be right back."

Dale's eyes widened. He held perfectly still, frozen in place.

Gritting his teeth, Adam broke eye contact and turned away. He clomped down the stairs, one boot still off and one on, and hit the exit door at a fast walk.

***

Once outside the door, the cold air hit him, and cleared his head immediately.

"Shit… shit… shit… shit… shit," he muttered, pacing in a circle, rubbing his face, hard. His stubble felt like sandpaper. He walked briskly off the concrete front porch and started into the parking lot, but the gravel was sharp and uncomfortable under his socked foot, so he came back to the patio and paced in anxious little circles.

"Think, Adam, think," he muttered. There was a rustic-looking wooden log bench next to the door, and he collapsed into it. "What are you gonna fuckin' do?" He wished he had a pack of cigarettes. Adam had never regularly smoked, only when he was really stressed out, and boy was he stressed out right now.

He had to admit the obvious: he was following in Dale's furry footsteps. It was obvious. He was getting all sorts of weird wolf-instinct feelings. Dominate him? That wasn't Adam's normal brain. Well… maybe a little. But more likely, he was clearly starting to turn. He thought about how Dale had scratched his arm, and the kiss, and the beers. He frowned. Any of those could have been the moment he got infected, but did it really matter how? The important thing was, it was happening. Whatever had happened to Dale, was happening to him.

Adam leaned forward. And yet—was that exactly true? "No, not really," he grumbled to himself. Dale had been sick all day, horribly so, and had undergone a terrifyingly violent transformation. Adam was just having weird intrusive thoughts. "Intrusive wolf-thoughts," he muttered. He got up and started pacing again.

Maybe he wasn't infected—maybe he had been exposed. Like when you have a brush with a cold and feel crappy for a few days but it never really hits you. Adam frowned into the night. Or like a… werewolf… vaccine? He pondered that for a moment before deciding he didn't really know what the hell he was talking about. He rubbed his face again, groaning. This was a lot for a county electrician to have to work his way through.

"Okay. Think," he said to himself. "Things got a little weird. But, you feel fine now." He thought about that. It was true. He looked down at his hands. Perfectly normal human hands. And, with appropriate distance, they might actually stay that way.

But Dale. Adam thought of him alone, upstairs. He was probably so upset. He swallowed. Adam wanted so bad to go back upstairs and just squeeze the poor monster until he felt better.

And what if he did? Would the wolf voice completely take over his brain? How long until the wolf body followed? Adam had a feeling the transformation wasn't far behind. He shuddered. Dale's change had been really rough.

Should he leave?

Adam pondered, grimacing. He glanced over his shoulder.

The county truck was right there.

He had the keys in his hand.

If he left now, he could call Kate on the way. She hadn't been exposed at all. She might have better luck interacting with Dale. He was docile now, over the worst of it. And that was probably the only way Adam was getting out of this with his humanity fully intact.

Adam stared at the truck.

Probably, he should leave.

He thought of the terrified wolf upstairs.

He blinked at it, looked down at the keys in his hand, and let out a long, irritated sigh.

Rolling his eyes, he turned back to the door of the ranger station.

He reached for the door knob. "I hope you appreciate this, Dale."

He put his hand on the knob.

Click-click.

Wide-eyed, Adam stared at it. He tried to turn it again. Click-click-click.

"Shit!" the big man hissed. Dale had warned him, and had to let him back in after his late dinner break. Make sure you get me— the door will lock behind you!

"Unggghhh!" Adam groaned. He took a couple steps back.

It took him another ten minutes to figure out how to get inside.

Overnight Shift

He decided not to call out to Dale, and none of the first-floor doors or windows were unlocked. Adam finally had to start up his truck, pull it around to the back deck, climb up on top of it, and scramble up the side of the deck like a 300-pound squirrel trying to get at a birdfeeder. He barely made it over the railing, the wood creaking under his feet, and dropped onto the deck with a grunt and a crash that shook the entire ranger station.

Panting, he took a moment to catch his breath.

His eyes settled on an object on the deck. Startled, he realized it was Dale's abandoned baseball cap.

His heart pounding, a lead weight of guilt dropping into his stomach, Adam crossed the deck to the sliding door and slipped his way in as fast as he could.

Eyes wide, he looked around. There was no sign of the wolf. Just signs of werewolf-related destruction.

Dale was being so silent that it took Adam a full thirty seconds to find him.

The wolf was on the sofa again, his head hidden facing the back of the couch, unmoving.

Adam leaned over him, panting. He stared at him. "Hey. Buddy. Are you okay? Dale, I'm back," he said, softly.

The wolf didn't respond.

Adam leaned over him so he could see his face. "Hey. Dale."

The wolf glanced cautiously back up at him, his golden eyes wide. "Arram?" he said, softly.

Adam felt his stomach clench. "Yeah," he said, softly. He frowned. "It's me. Who else would it be?"

Dale watched him, his brow furrowed. He frowned. "Hear truck," he said, softly, his ears flattening against his head. He looked... shaky. Nervous. Like he was trying to decide if Adam was real or not. Adam felt his heart grind like a bad transmission. Dale was being cautious. He was scared of him.

Adam swallowed. "I had to move it so I could climb onto the back deck. I locked myself out." He gave Dale a smile but it probably didn't look very convincing. He didn't feel like smiling. He felt terrible.

The wolf stared warily up at him. "Y-y-you don't leave?" he whispered.

Adam frowned. He didn't want to lie. "I... I thought about it," he admitted, guiltily. "I'm sorry. I was scared. But I didn't. I... couldn't." It was hard to get the words out. "Listen, I'm not gonna leave again, okay? I'm sorry."

Dale stared at him, and then nodded. He looked calm. Calm and relaxed. He stared at Adam for a long time before responding.

"Is okay," the wolf rumbled. "You came back," he pronounced, soberly.

Adam watched the animal, seeing the trust in his eyes, and realized he was speaking only to the animal side of Dale now. For the simple reason that human Dale would never, ever have given him a second chance.

The wolf watched him. It was that same dog-stare as before.

Adam cracked a smile. "Thanks for forgiving me, buddy." He reached for the wolf's muzzle. "C'mon, let's get these cords off of you." He gently rolled Dale onto his back.

Wide-eyed and silent, the wolf allowed Adam to remove the tied-off cord from the base of his muzzle. The fur was matted flat to the wolf's muzzle where the cord had been, so Adam gently ruffled it back up with his thumbs.

The wolf stared up at him while it was happening, and then slowly let his eyes drift shut in the same dazed, half-hypnotized expression as earlier. His unease melted away into blissful happiness, so Adam kept rubbing his muzzle, and finally the wolf let out a soft, contented sigh.

"You stay," the wolf whispered, contentedly.

With those words, Adam felt the bizarre pounding return to his heart. Dale was relaxed and docile in his arms. The wolf was his again. Adam started to feel good now, too, and it was only then that he realized how much it had upset him that the wolf was so distraught. Adam wanted to take care of him. He needed to. Why hadn't he seen it before? No wonder he had felt so panicked. The very thought of leaving his wolf behind had made him crazed. Now he felt calm and relaxed, too.

Gently closing his thick fingers around the wolf's muzzle, encircling it and holding it closed, Adam took a deep breath and pulled the animal closer toward him. He rubbed the wolf's head, ruffling his fur, playing with his huge fuzzy ears, and squeezing the wolf's muzzle and neck. He wasn't gentle, seeing how much the wolf would tolerate.

Dale arched his back, flaring his nostrils, and leaned into the ministrations. He lifted his upper lip for a moment, showing off a shocking flash of dangerous white teeth, before settling again. He half-closed his eyes and roughly nuzzled Adam's hands, and then he lifted his muzzle. He wasn't tolerating anything. He loved it.

Adam put his big hands around the animal's throat now, squeezing gently, digging his fingers into the muscle at the base of Dale's neck.

Now the wolf let out a noise that was somewhere between a whimper and a moan.

Adam stared. That had been an interesting sound. It made something burn deep inside him.

He thought for a moment. Everything was all right now. And they did have some time.

He dug his thumbs in at the base of Dale's jaw, leaning forward, and the big animal shivered in pleasure.

The wolf was absolutely his to do with as he wished now. Kate would be at least another two hours. Surely, there was nothing to be hurt by playing with his conquest… ?

Adam slid gently away from the wolf, taking the beast's bound wrists in his hands, and scooting off to his side. He pulled Dale-wolf's wrists upward, around his muzzle and up over his head. The wolf opened his eyes, baffled, and furrowed his brow, and his look of confusion only intensified when Adam tugged harder.

Cradling one arm under the smaller beast's back, Adam tugged him off the couch and laid him out on the hardwood. He pulled the wolf's arms taut over his head, pinning his wrists to the floor with one big hand. Scooting in next to him, he lay next to the prone wolf.

"How do you like this, Dale?" he rumbled, staring down at the animal. "Being laid out and helpless."

Dale bristled under his gaze, arching his back and opening his mouth. "H-hep-less?" He withered, his ears folding back against his head.

Adam could tell the dominant stare-down was making the wolf uncomfortable. He watched. But not bad-uncomfortable. Adam watched him. It was weird, he was so much more in-tune with Dale now, he could tell exactly what was going through the wolf's head.

Adam leaned forward. Still stubbornly refusing eye contact, the wolf began panting softly, his pink tongue poking out of his muzzle. He shivered, too, but it didn't seem like a scared shiver.

Adam let his eyes roam down and over the trapped ranger's form. He lifted his other hand and planted it on the wolf's barrel chest, feeling every feature of his thick, slab-like musculature. Dale arched his back and grunted, shivering, but Adam didn't stop. He dug his fingernails through the fur over the wolf's rigid stomach, making shallow furrows in the animal's shaggy fur.

Dale made a shuffling noise as he squirmed on the hardwood, gritting his teeth in discomfort. He glanced up at Adam, his golden eyes half-closed, showing a little teeth. It was a warning.

Adam snorted. "Oh no, Ranger Dale," he grunted. "I beat you fair and square, and now you're mine." He dragged his fingernails through Dale's chest fur, up toward the werewolf's throat. He felt strange, like he was watching from outside his body.

Dale arched his back and shivered, struggling to overpower Adam and bring his arms down, but only succeeded in tensing his stomach.

Staring him down, Adam let his big hand drift up to the wolf's throat. He planted his hand around Dale's neck, gently tightening his fingers, feeling his blood and heat and breath pulse through Dale's most vulnerable part. He tightened his grasp.

The ranger-wolf let out a strained whine, the edge of a growl in it.

Adam chuckled. "Don't worry, Dale, I'll be a good alpha." He let his gaze darken. "You've made my life miserable for a month, though. I think I need to make you squirm a little more." He gave the helpless werewolf's throat one more firm squeeze, and then let his hand slide down to gently massage the wolf's thick pecs. "You were kind of a prick, you know."

Dale glanced down at him and snorted, frowning. He stuck his lower lip out defiantly, and one of his lower fangs popped into view. You deserved it, the wolf said with the expression in his annoyed eyes.

Adam stared at him, and felt his upper lip twitching. "You disagree?" he said, cold as ice. "Well, little wolf, I'm afraid you're not in charge anymore." He grabbed Dale's bound wrists with both of his hands and lifted himself into a crouch. He scooted along the floor and pulled the werewolf along behind him.

The wolf yowled indignantly as the big electrician dragged him across the hardwood floor. He flailed his big digitigrade paws behind him, flapping and skittering on the floor, but he was no match for Adam's superior strength.

The larger human dragged the ranger to the back of the couch and shoved him toward one of its thick wooden legs. He dug his fingers in under the base of the sofa and heaved it upward an inch or two, surprised at how easy the giant old sofa was to lift. Stooping, he shoved the cord from Dale's furry wrists under the leg, and dropped it back into place, careful not to squash the ranger's paws in the process. Then he let go.

The thick black werewolf tried to pull his arms down as soon as he felt Adam's hands leave him, but discovered he was restrained by the couch a moment later. Squirming around to look at the couch leg he was bound to, the wolf let out a plaintive whine and yanked uselessly at his bonds. He glared. Now he was really mad.

Grinning, Adam moved around to the wolf's legs. He put one hand around each of Dale's thick ankles. Well—maybe they were his—upper feet? They were definitely joints, but Dale was digitigrade now, and his ankles were raised off the ground and much thicker. His actual paws were huge, as big as Adam's hands and considerably thicker, with thick leather pawpads and four wide fat toes.

Dale tried to pull his feet back, growling.

Adam narrowed his eyes, grinning savagely down at the animal. Dale was probably the sort of guy who hated people touching his feet. Dale-wolf was probably no different.

Adam pulled hard on the wolf's ankles, bringing his huge paws closer to his face. He leaned his face in, rubbing his beard up against Dale's paws.

The wolf arched his back and whined, opening his muzzle and showing his teeth.

Adam grinned savagely down at him. He leaned in and nibbled delicately at one of the ranger's pawpads. He tasted salt and then inhaled.

Dale writhed, straining as hard as he could to pull his feet away.

Adam stared down at him. He'd been expecting the usual corn-chip smell of dog paws, but that had been a dose of concentrated wolf musk. It left him feeling a little dizzy. His heart started pounding and for some reason he had the impulse to pin the wolf to the floor. He was also hard in his work pants, suddenly.

The wolf's eyebrows raised, as he sensed the change in Adam. He squirmed, gently, his ears tilting slowly backward.

Adam adjusted the wolf's ankles, scooting forward on his knees and bending Dale's knees back towards him. He kept moving forward, lifting the wolf's paws up over his head, the back of Dale's legs resting against Adam's chest as the human moved his crotch close to Dale's vulnerable fuzzy butt.

Dale watched him, confused, and then the wolf's eyes widened as the familiarity of the pose sunk in. This position would not be familiar to Wolf-Dale, but with whatever muscle memory remained of the wolf's human days, apparently he remembered. The wolf looked away with a very Dale-like look of embarrassment. Apparently, Dale was a bottom, which was not a terrific surprise.

Adam left the wolf's paws up and lowered his hands, brushing the backs of his fingers over Dale's vulnerable stomach.

Dale stared up at him, trusting and vulnerable, and Adam felt a weird stirring in his chest again. He was breathing harder now, his mouth partially open.

He encircled his plump sheath hanging out of the pulled down boxers. With his other hand, he slid his hands in underneath Dale's ass, and felt his balls through the wolf's boxers.

Dale jerked in surprise and stiffened, panting, pulling against his bound wrists. He gasped, showing his teeth again and snorting.

Adam narrowed his eyes. "Quit protesting," he growled. "I know exactly how you feel about this."

He took both his hands and put them around the wolf's boxers. He moved backward, roughly pulling the legs down and taking the boxers the rest of the way off. Dale shivered and fought weakly, but he wasn't really trying.

The boxers caught on his softball-sized paws. Dale pulled his legs back, glaring. Adam felt his upper lip rise and he pulled hard on the boxers.

Rrrrriiipppp! Dale's boxers finally gave way under Adam's strength, and split down the middle. Adam overbalanced sharply backward, but regained his balance almost immediately.

Dale was snarling at him now, writhing in discomfort, and only had a second to glare down at him before Adam lunged at him.

Baring his teeth, the big human roughly planted his mitt-like paws on the wolf's knees and spread his legs, hard.

"Yarp!" Dale yelped, his eyes widening in surprise, trying to double over and succeeding only in beautifully tensing his abs and dragging the couch a few inches with a deafening wood-on-wood squeal.

Adam thrust forward, diving his head toward Dale's vulnerable soft parts.

The wolf whined, loudly.

Laying practically on his stomach, braced on the wolf's tensed, spread legs, Adam stopped, perched half an inch over the wolf's exposed scrotum.

Wide-eyed and alarmed, the black wolf stared down at him, his ears cemented flat against his head.

Adam grinned and stared wild-eyed up at him.

Dale stared back at him, shivering, for another moment, and then averted his eyes, breathing hard. The wolf still looked pissed off, but he started squirming gently, and Adam saw his sheath start to plump up again.

He looked up at the wolf, who was now conspicuously avoiding eye contact, and Adam could smell him again. He stank of fear and submission, and of course that thick woodsy musk that Adam somehow now knew to be arousal.

Adam contemplated the wolf's balls and sheath for another moment, and then lowered his face to roughly nuzzle the wolf's fuzzy ballsac.

Dale jerked in surprise and tried to pull his legs back. He let out a shuddery breath, splaying his fat toes in discomfort. He was so vulnerable in this position. The sight made Adam's mouth water.

Adam nuzzled the wolf's dangling balls, opening his mouth and letting out a hot sigh. He dug his nose in against the base of Dale's fat sheath, and inhaled deeply. The wolf still smelled a lot like Dale, warm and soft and grizzly, and the scent made Adam's heart pound. Had he smelled Dale up-close before? He couldn't remember.

The wolf squirmed in discomfort, whimpering softly, and Adam felt bad for him, so he lifted his big left hand and planted it on the wolf's muscular stomach. He stroked gently, dipping his head and concentrating on the wolf's plump sheath, inhaling deeply, over and over again, letting out hot breaths over the wolf's fuzzy balls.

Dale grunted quietly, and the next time Adam looked up at the wolf, his mouth was partially open and he was watching again. Not defiantly, but intently, urgently. As Adam watched, the wolf's pink tongue poked slowly out, and Adam saw the wolf's barrel chest move like a mountain range as the ranger took a very deep breath.

He reached up with his right hand, too, and planted that one on Dale's stomach, as well, but he didn't stay put. He dragged his fingernails through Dale's shaggy fur down to the lowest expanse of his abdominals, and around the fat pronouncement of his sheath. He kept going, circling Dale's package, and gliding his fingers very gently under Dale's balls. He tickled him gently, playing with the werewolf's taint, softly nuzzling his sheath as he went.

Dale half-closed his eyes and shuddered extensively, arching his back and growling. He grit his teeth, pulling his upper lip back into

71

a snarl. The wolf's sheath was plump and heavy now, and Adam could see deep red within its confines as it began to open up.

Adam grasped the wolf's heavy balls and tugged them out of the way, dipping his head so he could nuzzle directly underneath the werewolf's dangling ballsac.

Dale arched his back and groaned loudly, and a wave of sweaty, acrid scent washed over Adam as the wolf's fat meat slid steadily out of his sheath.

Adam reached up for the wolf's meat as soon as it was in view. He started pumping it. The wolf's meat was the size of an energy drink can, maybe not quite as wide, but felt twice as heavy and scalding hot. As Adam worked him over, the wolf grew startlingly erect.

Dale arched his back harder, curling his shoulders in, tilting his head so far upward that Adam could only see the underside of his muzzle. Adam heard him whimper blissfully and the muscular wolf shuddered.

Licking his teeth, the big man raised his head. "How's that feel, Dale?" he whispered, working the wolf's dick over. It was deep red, like blood, with a normal head but a strong taper at the tip. The base seemed to have a thick bulge in it, which was getting thicker.

Dale gasped loudly. "Ahhdam!" he moaned, shivering violently. His voice had an edge of a desperate howl in it.

He'd said his name. Unprompted, no less. Adam felt something like electricity move through him.

"Good boy," Adam rumbled.

Panting, the wolf looked down at him, his golden eyes wide and apprehensive. "G… good?" he gasped, shivering violently.

Adam licked his teeth, and nodded. "Yeah, Dale," he whispered, leaning his head forward and taking the wolf's fat cock into his mouth. He pursed his lips and sucked, hard.

"Aaaaahh!" Dale gasped, jerking as if hurt. Adam held him down by the hips, and the wolf struggled as if trying to escape.

Inhaling through his nose, Adam relaxed his mouth around the wolf's dick and slid lower. It was almost shockingly hot, heavy and large, and it filled Adam's mouth pleasantly. He sucked hard, lowering his head until the head of Dale's monster wolf cock was lodged firmly in the back of his throat, feeling his mouth fill with slimy fluids as the wolf's throbbing member leaked milky precum into his throat. He swallowed, rumbling.

"Howroorooroo!" Dale yowled, writhing and gasping. Every muscle in his body was tense and squirming now, and the wolf burned with a ferocious amount of energy. And yet he was helpless to escape. He didn't want to escape anymore, Adam knew.

That thought made his skin feel like it was on fire.

He sucked the trapped wolf for a long time, holding him perfectly still, pinned down to the floor, laid out for Adam's gratification. The sensations didn't seem to ease for the wolf so much as intensify, Adam could tell by the beast's increasingly desperate squirming.

There was one more thing left to do.

Still nursing the wolf's fat meat, Adam let his thick fingers slip between the wolf's legs.

Dale squirmed blissfully under his ministrations until the moment Adam had his middle finger planted right up against the wolf's asshole, and then he realized what was about to happen. He tensed his entire body, inhaling sharply.

Adam pushed his thick middle finger into the wolf as hard as he dared without lube. He forced his way into the wolf's entrance easily, sliding in deep.

"Arrrrrp!" Dale yelped, jerking hard enough to rattle the trinkets on the nearby bookshelves. He writhed, his thick toeclaws skittering on the hardwood, but he was too startled and uncoordinated to move himself anywhere.

Adam slid off the wolf's cock, slurping up the excess fluids. "Ssssshhh," he whispered, stroking the wolf's stomach with his other hand. He nuzzled the wolf's slimy, drooling cock, smearing wolf juice and his own spit into his stubble, staring Dale right in the eye as he did it.

Dale writhed in discomfort, gritting his teeth and whimpering.

Adam curled his finger inside the wolf, roughly massaging the inside of his asshole, whispering to him as he nuzzled and kissed at his throbbing cockhead.

The werewolf watched him helplessly for another few moments, breathing hard and fast, and then slowly he fell victim to the dull waves of pleasure washing over him.

"That's it," Adam rumbled. "Give in, little wolf. Show me you're really mine." He sucked gently on the sticky saliva-coated ridge of the wolf's cockhead, suckling softly, nuzzling it lovingly.

Dale blinked slowly, letting out a slow breath, and Adam felt him relax his asshole. He held his finger in place, massaging the wolf's insides with slow, rhythmic, gentle pressure. The wolf stared stupidly down at him, his mouth opening slowly, and his tongue lolling out. He shivered in pleasure, and somewhere underneath him must have been a loose floorboard, because it went CLAKCLAKCLAK! when the wolf's leg shook.

Adam kept working at it, and to his surprise, Dale went mostly limp. Lying flat on his back, he lifted his knees up but otherwise he was completely motionless. He let out a soft, shaky moan, and simply lay there, giving in to his bondage, and letting the bigger man penetrate him. He shivered, breathing hard now, and his cock stood rigidly over his belly.

Adam watched him, witnessing the wolf's complete and total surrender, and licked his teeth.

"Hey," he said, his voice an octave deeper than it should have been.

Eyes half-closed, the wolf raised his head to stare at him with half-focused eyes.

Adam swallowed. "I'm going to mount you now," he said, quietly.

Dale stared back at him, his eyes suddenly clearing, and nodded.

Adam grunted. "Wait here," he ordered. He slid his finger out of the wolf and stood up.

Dale grimaced, but he didn't make a sound.

***

It only took Adam a few seconds to dig the Astroglide out of the bottom section of his toolbox, but when he got back it was like he was seeing Dale for the first time.

The wolf had finally freed his wrists from the bonds that held him, which was not very interesting to Adam, since he was completely confident of the wolf's obedience.

What caught his attention was the black wolf's size and power, his muscular perfection, his jaws massive and dangerous and dripping with saliva. He glared at Adam, a perfect killing machine, a true monster. He looked like he could go up against an entire SWAT team and come out on top.

But Adam knew the truth.

As soon as he was close enough, he dropped to his knees and lunged at the wolf, pinning him to the floor and flipping him onto his belly. The wolf struggled, and he was strong, but Adam was stronger, which meant that the other animal was as good as his pet.

"Hold still, little wolf," Adam snarled, raising himself to his knees, digging his fingers into the wolf's ruff with one hand and frantically wrestling open his work pants with the other. Dale yelped indignantly, writhing back against him, as Adam manhandled his own cock out of his jeans. Adam was a solid eight or nine inches long, and thick as a nightstick, making him considerably bigger than Dale in every category. He could barely get his dick out of his underwear, he was already so hard, and he had leaked so much precum into his briefs that his dick was already slick and sticky.

He struggled to uncap the lube as Dale writhed underneath him. Grunting, he dropped his weight onto the smaller wolf. Dale yelped loudly as he was pinned to the floor. Adam ground his cock up under the wolf's tail but he wasn't lubed yet.

Awkwardly, he rolled partially onto his side, still pinning Dale down with all his weight, squirted lube over his cock like he was trying to empty the tube, and ran his hand up and down his cock a few times.

Dale turned his head around and snarled loudly, foam collecting at the corner of his mouth. He had all the hallmarks of anger but Adam could tell by looking at him that the monster was just really keyed up.

Grinning evilly, Adam dug his middle finger under the wolf's tail and into his ass.

"Yarrrrp!" Dale yelped, writhing in his grasp. Adam lubed him up from the inside out, enjoying the feel of the muscular wolf's tensing, struggling ass.

Snarling back, Adam rolled back over and thrust at the wolf's ass.

It wasn't gracious or elegant. It was pure, feral animal lust. He had to jab two or three times before he finally found his target and speared the wolf's asshole.

Dale jerked in shock underneath him, gasping, and Adam felt him start to yield. Then Adam really let him have it.

He thrust forward, sliding inch after inch into the wolf, much harder and faster than he would ever have dared to fuck a human. He threw his left arm around the wolf's neck in a headlock again and pulled him backward, holding Dale steady as the wolf was slowly impaled. Dale's ass fur tickled Adam's cock the entire time he was sliding in, and when he finally hilted in, his fluffy butt tickled the electrician's bare lap.

"ARRRRRRRRRPPPP!" Dale cried. He clenched, but Adam didn't stop. The wolf's entire body stiffened, but he was no longer struggling.

Grunting, buried in the wolf up to the hilt, Adam shifted on top of the conquered monster. He felt shaggy fur pressing against the entire front of his body, pinned underneath him, and it felt amazing. It just felt so right. He was dizzy and hot and horny. His heart was racing and his cock was surrounded by warm, wet werewolf. He held Dale tight, buried inside him.

Dale shivered underneath him, and they both took a moment, breathing hard, Adam towering over the conquered beast.

Experimentally, he reached up underneath the werewolf, his hand still smeared with lube. He found Dale half-hard, and played gently with him, working the wolf back up to full hardness.

Dale writhed under the ministrations, somewhere between uncomfortable and aroused. He squirmed, clenching his asshole around Adam's invading member, and the big man shivered on top of and inside him.

76

Setting his jaw, Adam gently pulled a few inches out of the werewolf, getting his bearings before pushing quickly back into him.

Dale grunted and dipped his head underneath him.

Adam tightened the headlock with his left arm, bringing Dale's shaggy head up to his face, and he nuzzled the werewolf's muzzle. Some of his facial fur was wet with slick wolf drool, and the sensation of nuzzling a hot, wet werewolf muzzle made Adam feel dizzy. His cock throbbed inside the captive animal as he adjusted to the sensation of being mouth-to-muzzle with a wolf. It felt... right.

Shivering, Dale hung his tongue out, panting gently.

Watching the wolf intently, Adam pushed his hips forward a little.

"Nnf!" Dale chuffed. He retracted his tongue and grit his teeth.

Adam rumbled, clearing his throat. "You can take it," he said, huskily. He dug his cock into the flattened wolf again.

Dale grit his teeth, squeezing his eyes shut, and shivered. "Nnnnf!" he gasped, softly.

Adam pressed his beard against the wolf's shaggy muzzle, digging into him again.

Dale shivered again, half-opening his mouth now. He was starting to enjoy it.

Adam rumbled, opening his mouth, too. "I knew you'd love this," he whispered. "I love it, too. You're such a good boy." It felt good to say it. He started humping gently at the helpless monster.

Dale let out a rough breath and sucked in another, his eyes still closed, opening his mouth wider. He'd given Adam a chance. He was being such a good wolf. He deserved a reward.

On impulse, Adam licked at the short fur of Dale's black muzzle. It felt like something a wolf would like. It would show him Adam was being affectionate. It would show him he was right to submit. He expected the sensation to be strange, but it wasn't. Dale's muzzle was warm, his fur was bristly, and the slimy sheen of saliva felt... amazing.

The wolf angled his head and licked Adam back, slurping across his lips and the end of his nose. He exhaled shakily as he did it, his yellow eyes half-closed and dreamy, and Adam could feel the wolf's thick canine teeth graze his lips.

He pushed his hips forward, harder and faster than he had before, and Dale stiffened beneath him. "Ngh!" the werewolf grunted.

Adam thrust into him again, and again, and as Dale shoved his muscular furry ass back against the electrician, they finally settled into a rhythm, one that Adam had desired since he'd first laid eyes on the ranger a month ago.

Their rhythm was swift and brutal, almost the same pace Adam set for himself when he was exercising, one he wouldn't have guessed he'd have been able to maintain. He ground himself into the helpless wolf over and over again, fast and shallow, both of them nearly immobile except for Adam's hips, spearing the wolf anew every few seconds.

As he mated the animal, Adam pinned him to the floor, crushing his legs and chest underneath him, holding him down. With his tongue he entered the wolf from the other end, and Dale allowed him to, submitting entirely without resistance, giving himself completely to the bigger animal. All teeth and claws and muscle, the wolf simply lay there, and took it.

"Yeah... yeah... yeah... yeah... yeah..." Adam groaned, his brutal humping of the werewolf growing more and more frenzied. He felt his leg muscles start to burn from his tenuous stance on the hardwood, and his ass starting to burn from the ferocious humping he was doing. It was a good burn, and it excited him more. He kept going.

"Nnnrrrggghhh!" Dale yowled, gritting his teeth and snorting loudly. "Arr..dam!" he gasped, tilting his head to the side and squeezing his eyes shut. He was baring his throat.

An insane impulse roared into Adam's head, and he lunged forward to sink his teeth into the scruff at the back of the werewolf's neck, biting him and yanking his head back hard. Dale let out an ear-splitting yelp.

Suddenly, something started to change.

It began in his hands. There was a burning-hot sensation, like his hands had gone to sleep and were just starting to regain feeling.

The muscles in his hands and forearms twitched and spasmed, and for a moment it felt like when he accidentally shocked himself with a live wire. Exactly like that feeling, complete with the momentary numbness and pins-and-needles a moment later, and that was when Adam realized what was happening.

His hands grew larger in a matter of seconds, and the explosion of fur started immediately after. His skin felt like it was sliding off, and then his entire body went completely numb at the same time. Adam felt light-headed and dizzy, little white stars exploding across his field of vision, and when he regained feeling it was like he was in someone else's body. Every single skin receptor in his body reported fur rubbing against more fur, and for a moment, his skin was crawling as Adam tensed up from head to toe.

The skeletal changes coursed through him with a sensation unlike anything he had ever felt before, a peculiar combination of needing to crack every joint in his body and a bizarre, unstoppable swelling. Adam felt himself get big, and he sucked in a deep breath in his massive chest. He snarled viciously, the deep growl filling the ranger's station, and Dale whined in fear underneath him.

His right foot felt incredibly compressed for a moment, intense pain bordering on agony, and then with a tearing sound suddenly the pressure was released. His boot loosened to the point where it just felt like strips of leather and shreds of cloth draped loosely around his foot. And then Adam realized, it was just strips of leather and shreds of cloth. His foot had exploded his one remaining construction-grade boot. His toes felt big and thick, positively massive, and they were stuck in the wreckage of his boot, but it didn't affect his stance over the smaller wolf, who he was still skewering.

The muzzle and tail happened at the same time, and they were both so bizarre—nerves where there were none, and the insane sensation of a spinal extension—that he actually blacked out for a moment. His nervous system simply couldn't process the change, and the world went dark for a moment as his view cascaded abruptly to blackness.

**

When his brain kicked back on, the massive wolf was very disoriented. He growled loudly, his head spinning, snorting loudly. There was another wolf near him. No, underneath him. He had the other wolf flattened beneath his massive bulk. He felt a warm, wet tongue on his thick, wide muzzle, slurping lovingly and submissively, and with that he knew everything would be fine. The large wolf opened his eyes and blinked slowly.

Pack. He was with pack. The smaller black wolf underneath him was known to him, and the lesser beast continued licking his muzzle. It made the large wolf relax, even though, for some reason, his own white muzzle seemed to absolutely fill his frame of vision. He was so disoriented. The color white looked wrong. Why?

"Arram?" whispered his packmate, and the big wolf knew his name.

Relieved to be in the company of a known wolf, the big animal leaned and nuzzled his black packmate, and the smaller wolf shivered in pleasure. No… ecstasy. He could smell it. "Arram," the smaller beast moaned, and the scent of arousal pouring off of him made the larger wolf's cock throb to attention. As his cock returned to hardness, Adam was startled to realize he was already inside the smaller wolf.

Adam leaned in to roughly nuzzle the smaller wolf's thick neck, and the small beast's name came back to him. He slurped Dale's face, growling softly, and bit gently at the submissive wolf's muzzle, feeling himself grow to full hardness inside the other wolf. His heart was pounding. He barely knew what was going on, but it was clear that they had been mating. He intended to continue.

Dale dipped his muzzle, whining softly, his tongue hanging out. "Bigger," he grunted, gritting his teeth, but Adam didn't know what that meant so he did what his body commanded him to. He pushed as deep as he could into the wolf, breathing hard, feeling his own big muscles working as if for the first time, his thick tail lashing bizarrely behind him. The only sensation he cared about was the sensation of impaling the smaller wolf on his invading meat.

After a moment, the smaller wolf's ruff found its way into his mouth, and Adam closed his teeth around it, and with his dick inside his packmate and his head full of endorphins, Adam felt happy and high.

Experimentally, he slid his dick a small measure out of his trapped packmate, and thrust it forward again.

Dale whined loudly, pushing back up against him, dipping his head with his tongue hanging out.

Adam repeated the motion, harder, and harder still.

Dale pushed faithfully back against him, his pawpads and claws barely holding him in place, his legs shivering hard as Adam spread him open and filled him. The little wolf shuddered underneath him, and Adam rumbled, pleased. The smaller animal was overcome with pleasure, on the verge of total release.

Very well.

Adam bucked his hips as hard as he dared, his jaws clenched around Dale's thick scruff, crushing the wolf between his teeth and his cock. The thickened base of his wolfhood spread Dale as wide as he had ever been opened, and then suddenly the thick knot in the base of Adam's cock popped into the smaller wolf and stayed there. Underneath him, he felt Dale jerk violently in surprise.

"Yarrrp!" the little wolf grunted as he was plugged tight, shivering violently in place, completely helpless even to move now. He squirmed, caught. Adam knew by his scent that the little wolf was on the very edge of climax himself, but now that he was tied, the smaller animal would be helpless to speed the process along. Dale hung his head and moaned desperately, his eyes half-shut and his tongue hanging out.

Adam bucked shallowly against him, inhaling deeply and snarling involuntarily. The sensations began to build within him, of Dale's ass clamped around his knot combined with the lesser lupine's muscular body squirming against his stomach, chest, and thighs, and Adam felt like his chest was going to burst open.

Squeezing the impaled wolf in a crushing embrace, Adam grit his teeth and bore down, digging his muzzle into Dale's shoulder as his bestial lust completely took over.

"Awrooooooooooooooooooooooooo!" Adam howled, feeling his cock twitch and jerk inside the smaller wolf, and he could feel himself pouring into the other animal, the sensation shooting up into his brain and making his fingers and toes tingle. He lost control of his arms and legs, squeezing the smaller wolf with crushing force. Adam grit his teeth, snarling, squeezing his eyes shut as his orgasm hit him so hard it was almost painful. He poured his seed into the smaller wolf.

Writhing in the larger wolf's grasp, Dale whined sharply, his eyes opening wide and alarmed, and he shivered violently under the big wolf. He yanked his head back, hitting the underside of Adam's chin, hard, and howled as he shook with his own climax. "Hawroooooo!" Dale yowled, clinging to Adam's thick forearms, his unattended cock gushing thick gobs of wolf semen all over the floor, and into his stomach and chest fur, all the way up to the underside of both of their muzzles. He bucked his hips shallowly, his strong body jerking under Adam's, but unable to get anywhere.

Still filling the little wolf from the inside, Adam began to lose feeling in his thick fingers and hands. His meat just kept unloading into the helpless little wolf trapped in his grasp, for a long, long time, filling him, as his little black packmate squirmed and clenched around his invading member.

The little wolf finished first, shuddering as if freezing, quivering uncomfortably and whining loudly. He clung to Adam like he was scared of being torn away from him.

The massive wolf on top felt his cock finally relax, and then it was like all the strength went out of his body. He couldn't move his arms even to release the little wolf from his tight grip, so he simply went limp. Let the little wolf take it from here, he thought. He trusted him.

They tilted over to the side. Dale grunted. Adam simply exhaled.

The smaller wolf shivered for a good full minute after they were finished. Adam held him tightly and positioned his muzzle to lick the side of Dale's muzzle. He tasted content and relaxed.

There was something else floating around in Adam's mind. Something to do. Or… prepare for?

He blinked his now-yellow eyes, frowning, and stared into the night. What… how… what did… .

Dale shivered again, letting out a soft, contented whine, and craned his head to affectionately lick the underside of Adam's muzzle.

Adam remembered this wolf was his to protect, and nothing mattered beyond that. He held guard over him the best way he knew how: he held him tightly in his arms.

That was all Adam could remember, so he kicked off the strange pieces of fabric clinging to his paws, made a conscious decision to ignore the fabric coverings around his legs, rested his head on his packmate's neck, and closed his eyes.

In just a few seconds, he fell sound asleep.

***

6:44 AM

Daylight was just beginning to fill the sky when Kate Campbell made it to the ranger station.

She pulled in, taking care to point the nose end of her CR-V back toward the main road. The gravel crackled under her tires as she piloted the car to face the parking lot's exit. She would have a quick escape if she needed one.

Kate hated to think why she might need such a thing, but her mother hadn't raised an idiot, and when she was walking into a situation like "Don't bring the authorities or we'll never see him again," it wasn't hard to theorize that she might need to leave the ranger station at a full run. Kate mulled this over as she tied her red hair behind her head in a ponytail.

She unclipped her station keys and scrambled out of the Honda, leaving the car running and the driver's door standing open behind her. Walking briskly to the front door, her heart pounding with adrenaline, she looked around.

Dale's truck was still there. So was Adam's, though it was weirdly parked under the back deck. Neither vehicle showed signs of being disturbed. There were no car keys or articles of clothing lying abandoned in the gravel driveway. No blood stains. Looking up at the building, she detected no broken windows or bullet holes. So far, so good.

Tightening her right hand around the pepper spray in her purse, Kate unlocked the front door. She opened it loudly.

As soon as she entered she heard scrambling near the top of the stairs.

"Who's there?" she called, loudly.

"Oh shit!" she heard Adam say, huskily, on the main floor. Not a great sign. His voice sounded deep, like he had just woken up.

"I'm coming up," Kate announced, stepping toward the stairs.

There was a scramble of rustling and thumping at the top of the stairs.

Withdrawing the pepper spray, Kate started up the steps. She pressed herself toward the right side, edging up with her back against the wood-paneled exterior wall, her pepper spray raised and her finger on the trigger.

Adam and Dale weren't hard to find. Their condition, however, was altogether unexpected.

Adam Chaney stood a few yards inside the entrance, his shirt off, his pants open and unbuttoned and… torn, ripped in jagged tears down both of his thighs? He was frantically buckling the belt on what was left of his dust-covered khaki work pants, and when his thick bare arms moved in certain ways, Kate could just make out Dale cowering deeper in the room. In the occasional flashes of Dale, she saw bare skin and black hair and absolutely nothing else.

Kate stared, her mouth hanging open.

"G'morning!" Adam said, cheerfully.

"It's not what it looks like!" Dale cried from behind him.

Kate cocked her head and stared at them. Yep. Adam and Dale. Clearly getting dressed.

Adam considered, glancing back at Dale. "Actually, the part that you're probably thinking of is totally what it looks like." He grinned a big stupid goofy grin back at the ranger.

Kate couldn't see much of Dale, but she did catch him glaring daggers back at Adam.

She frowned sourly. "Alright, you imbeciles. There's nobody else here? Nobody's in mortal peril?"

Adam shook his head.

Kate rolled her eyes. "Put some clothes on and start explaining." She turned around, facing the entrance stairwell. "You have ten seconds."

There was a frantic rustling behind her.

Sighing, Kate felt like she was back in college and she'd walked in on her roommate having sex with some fratboy moron.

"It's really not what it looks like!" Dale wailed pathetically.

Adam chuckled, a deep bass. "Dude, you gotta stop saying that."

Eight... nine... ten. "Time's up." Kate whirled around.

Dale was still bare-chested and barely wearing his hunter-green work pants (minus any undergarments, Kate noticed), facing away from her, and he yelped pitifully as his thick legs fought the canvas. He toppled over onto the couch, eyes wide and alarmed, crimson from the middle of his chest up to the top of his head. Adam, on the other hand, leisurely picked a white shirt off the coffee table and handed it to Dale. "Hi!" he greeted Kate, brightly.

Kate stared at him, and then looked down at the electrician's thick and muscular chest. He wasn't hard on the eyes. "Leave the shirt off," she said. "I at least deserve a little eye candy for getting dragged out here."

Adam processed that and then grinned at her like a labrador. If he had a tail it would be wagging, she thought.

"Now then. You want to tell me what the hell happened? I assume your sexcapades weren't the reason for the twenty frantic phone calls last night." She looked back and forth between the dopey electrician and the cowering ranger. Dale scrambled off the couch and paced around, looking for his shoes and socks. "You can't even find your clothes? You idiots must've fucked like animals in here."

Adam's grin actually increased in size. He tried to exchange a glance at Dale, who turned a deeper shade of crimson and very deliberately avoided his gaze.

Overnight Shift

Dale pulled his shirt over his head, swallowing. "It's nothing," the ranger grunted, his voice low and angry. "We had a few drinks. Got to foolin' around. May have made some unnecessary phone calls." He glared at Adam, and then turned back to Kate. "Sorry to ruin your evening."

Kate narrowed her eyes at him, and Dale practically shriveled before her gaze.

Dale lowered his head like a scolded dog. He wouldn't meet her eyes.

Adam cleared his throat. "Dale's a werewolf," he said, simply.

Wide-eyed, Dale stood there, petrified.

It took Kate's brain a moment to process the words that Adam had spoken. She looked up at him very slowly. "I'm sorry," she said. "What was that?"

The big electrician cocked his head. "Dale's a werewolf, and he turned into this beast thing, and then he turned ME into a beast thing, and then we had sex." He stared at them. "Crazy, wild, man-beast sex." He nodded, thoughtfully. "We thought he had the flu, but he actually had... werewolfism."

Kate stared at him, and then at Dale, and then back at Adam, and then back at Dale. Adam looked smug and vaguely dopey— normal, in other words—and Dale looked horrified, down to his very core. Neither one of them seemed particularly amused.

Kate slid her pepper spray slowly back out of her purse.

Adam's eyes widened. "Whoa, hey!" he said. "I didn't say we were dangerous!"

Kate narrowed her eyes. "I don't think you are. I am very dangerous, however!" She pointed the pepper spray at Adam. "And if you idiots think it's funny that I drove eighty-five miles at five in the morning on no sleep for a fucking prank, you do not know the meaning of the word dangerou-"

Adam cut her off, waving his big hands in front of her. "No, seriously!" he gasped. "I mean it! Dale, tell her!" He turned to the ranger.

Head hunched down, Dale swallowed, frowning. He glanced over to glare at Adam. He looked... torn.

"It's okay," Adam said, softly. "I got you, man." He smiled encouragingly.

Dale stared at him for a long time, and finally rolled his eyes, sighing. Another few moments passed with agonizing slowness. He looked away. "I don't know what I got to tell her that you didn't already," he whispered.

Kate stared at them both. "Oh, please." She was still holding the pepper spray, but she couldn't decide which of them to point it at.

Adam grunted. "You're right. It's much more likely that Dale charmed a handsome bisexual twenty-something with eighteen-inch biceps and literally dozens of other sexual prospects, because he's such a smooth guy."

Kate thought about that, and slowly lowered the pepper spray. "Okay," she said. "I suppose you do have a point there."

Dale furrowed his brows angrily. "Hey!"

She turned toward Adam. "I'm only entertaining this thought because I haven't slept in twenty-eight hours and I am running on gas station coffee, but I'm gonna need more proof than that."

Adam nodded, and then looked around. It only took him a moment. "Here," he said, taking two steps and reaching down for something.

It was a construction boot, a big one, 16 at least. It definitely looked like Adam's. Or at least, it looked like it had been Adam's, because the leather upper was separated from the rubber sole, which was nowhere to be found. It looked like the boot had burst from within, like someone had inflated a car airbag inside of it. Frayed yellow switching hung from the mangled leather boot-top like dangling jungle vines.

Kate stared at the boot, and two thoughts popped into her head. The first, was Hey! That's a great prop for such a lame prank! The other, was Holy shit, they're telling the truth!

She cocked her head. "Great prop. Got anything else?" She felt surprisingly calm about the entire thing.

Adam looked around. "How about that?" He gestured toward the break room door.

Kate stared at that a moment. The door had clearly been destroyed. Bits of it were scattered all around the floor. Half of the door was still attached to the hinges but it had been splintered, vertically, and the ends looked like it had been chewed off by an industrial scrapping machine. In fact, the entire station was destroyed. There were bits of broken glass scattered amid piles of books and pamphlets. Two of the tables were flattened, actually flattened, laying in crushed heaps with the remains of several computers laid out over and near them. Sunlight streamed in through torn-down miniblinds. Kate could see broken glass in the large window behind them.

She stared.

Again, that voice. This is not a prank, it said.

She frowned. "Jesus. I mean… hmm." Quickly, she shook her head. "No, that could still have been your psychosexual Olympics." She turned back to him. "Got anything better?"

Dale let out a strangled whine, and the sound was so undeniably lupine that it made the hairs on the back of Kate's neck stand up. "Katie, you don't believe this shit, do you?" he whimpered. He looked back at Adam and back at her, hunching his shoulders anxiously. He even held himself like a scared dog.

She watched him.

Those sounds.

Kate had spent three weeks of her thesis research period on the wolves at the Louisville Zoo, and the noise Dale had just made… it was uncanny.

Could they actually be…?

"Hold on, I think I got something better," Adam grunted.

Kate glanced at Adam but turned back to frown at Dale.

Breathing hard, he stared back. He was terrified. Was there something to this?

"Ngh!" Adam suddenly grunted, and Kate heard what sounded like knuckles popping crazy-loud, and when she turned back, her rational brain took a little vacation.

Adam was looking down at his hands, except they weren't his hands anymore. They were gigantic white-furred wolf-paws. Except they weren't exactly paws, they were more like hand-paws, all the way down to the elbows, and yep, that man was definitely a werewolf. He looked at his paws and grinned, satisfied.

Dale gasped too. "D-did that hurt? Are you okay?" he gaped.

Adam grinned at him. "I told you I got this, man."

Kate stared at the two of them, and felt strangely calm. "Okay," she said. "I guess that will do it." She turned back to Dale. "How long have you been a werewolf and didn't tell me? That's very hurtful, Dale." She felt drunk.

Dale stared pathetically at both of them, dipping his head and hunching over anxiously. He looked nervously back and forth, his eyes wide, like he might make a break for it.

Adam straightened up, eyes wide. "Hey, it's okay," he said, soothingly. "Kate's a friend. She's gonna help us figure this thing out." He crossed the room to Dale in three steps, and just when Kate thought the ranger was going to bolt, Adam put his furry arms around him. He held him tight and slid around behind him.

As Kate watched, Dale visibly calmed. Adam pressed his bare chest up to the ranger's back, and Dale took a few deep breaths. He blinked as if in surprise, breathing deeply, and before thirty seconds had passed he was all but asleep in Adam's arms.

"It's all right," Adam whispered into Dale's ear, nuzzling the back of his head, squeezing him gently. Dale reached up to gently touch Adam's furry forearms, looking relaxed and subdued.

Kate watched the two of them, and then the scientist part of her brain finally spoke up. "Oh, my God. Are you guys like… bonded?"

Adam looked up at her, wide-eyed and clueless. Dale hung his head, frowning in shame. He clearly didn't want to be part of an impromptu pack. But, he didn't deny that he was.

A torrent of information began roiling through Kate's brain, consisting of basically every piece of lupine-related information she remembered from ten different biology courses. Now, her curiosity began to get the better of her.

She took ten steps to snatch a magnifying glass off of one of the exam tables and strode over to Adam and Dale with it. "Palm up," she said.

Blinking in confusion, and then grinning like an idiot, Adam lifted his big white-furred right paw and opened his fingers.

It was undeniably, impossibly real, right in front of her. Hand and finger structures were notoriously difficult to replicate, even for big-budget film studios, and Kate could tell immediately that she was looking at a piece of a living organism, skin, fur, tendons and all.

She grasped the back of Adam's paw with one hand—which was huge, it was like holding a throw pillow—moderately surprised at how soft and warm it was. She peered over his palm with her glass at hand.

The leather was fine-grained and authentically paw leather in structure. Adam waggled his fingers and she saw the leather wrinkle and stretch. There was a wide, variegated scar spanning across the flat of his palm.

"Mmm," she said. "Is this a scar you… normally have?" She looked up at him.

Adam blinked at her. "I grabbed a saucepan off the stove," he said. "When I was six."

"Interesting," Kate said again, leaning down. She glanced at Dale. "Did your transformation go like this too?"

Dale stared at her, wide-eyed. Silently, he shook his head.

"No way, man," Adam supplemented. "When he turned it was a horror show. I thought he was like dying."

Dale frowned. He looked away. "It was pretty bad," he said, quietly.

Kate frowned grimly at him. Dale had once fallen off a ladder and impaled a screwdriver completely through the webbing of his left hand, and described the situation as "unpleasant." For him to call his condition "pretty bad" probably warranted an ambulance.

She turned to Adam. "God. How bad did he get?"

Adam thought for a moment. "Did you ever see Aliens?"

Kate stared at him.

Dale narrowed his eyes. "It wasn't that bad."

Adam shook his head. "Yes, it was. I finished working at like two in the morning, but I stuck around another couple hours because he looked so bad. I didn't want to leave him alone."

They both blinked at him. Slowly, Kate turned to look at Dale.

The older ranger's jaw was hanging open in undisguised shock, and after a moment he clamped his jaw shut and turned crimson. Adam just grinned at him. Dale glowered.

Kate shook her head. "So, he changed involuntarily?" She gathered some of Adam's thick white fur in her hand and tugged, hard.

"OW! YES!" Adam snapped. He writhed. "Cut that out!"

Kate frowned. "Don't be such a baby." She had a couple furs in her hand and set them aside for later analysis. Hopefully they hadn't destroyed all the microscopes. "So, Dale turned first. How did you get exposed?" She frowned. "I should probably be wearing gloves. I hope you're not still contagious."

Adam chuckled. "I dunno, man. I drank out of his beer bottle. I handled him when he was all sweaty. And, he scratched me up pretty bad when he changed. And uh, also, we, uh, made out for a bit. And then, uhhh… I fucked 'im." He grinned, sheepishly.

Dale writhed out of Adam's grasp and loped silently a few feet away.

Kate stared at him. "You fucked… a werewolf," she said, slowly.

Adam frowned. "Well, like… we had already kissed. It's not like there wasn't a precedent."

Kate narrowed her eyes. "You kissed a werewolf?"

Adam frowned. "No, he was HUMAN then."

Kate dropped her jaw. "You kissed when you were both human?"

Adam frowned. "Yeah," he said. "We had a couple drinks though." He frowned. "It's, uh, not a good story." He shook his head.

They both glanced at Dale, who was conspicuously avoiding eye contact and looking like he wanted to climb onto the roof to escape the conversation.

Kate shook her head. "So, you kissed, he changed, and then you fucked a supernatural being?" She frowned. "Did you use protection?!"

Adam shook his head.

Kate reached up and slapped his bald head. "See? This is why we'll never have sex, you dumbass! You didn't use a condom and now you caught werewolf!"

Adam growled at her. "Hey! It's not MY fault!" He shrugged. "I dunno, man, I think I already had it by then. All I could think about was dominating him."

They both turned to look at Dale, who again seemed to shrink before them.

Kate nodded. "Interesting. Explain."

Adam shrugged. "I dunno. I was already feeling pretty protective, and I definitely was already into him. But, when I decided to stay I felt like…" He trailed off. "I couldn't think of anything besides making him like… submit to me so I could protect him. I had all these weird impulses to pin him down, and at one point I just kind of… bit him." He licked his teeth in a gesture that Kate had never seen before.

Kate frowned. She raised a questioning eyebrow. "Sounds… kind of horny?"

Adam nodded, eyes wide. "Oh, yeah!" he confirmed, excited. "It was SUPER horny."

"Fascinating." She turned to Dale.

He shook his head, his mouth open. "Don't look at me," he growled. "I could barely remember my own name."

Kate turned back to the bigger man and Adam was staring at the ranger, cracking a smile. "He's still smaller than me, even as a wolf. Taller and bigger than normal, but not bigger than me." He puffed his chest out, watching the ranger predatorily. "He rolled over pretty easily."

Kate nodded. Dale blushed.

They were silent for a moment.

Kate frowned. "Okay. Here's the deal. I agree with Adam that we can't call the authorities or you'll both end up in Area 51. We need to find out what this is, if it's going to continue to spread, and I really need to figure out how Dale got it in the first place." She turned. "I assume you would have mentioned it if you were attacked by a wolf in the last few days."

Dale blinked at her, and frowned tightly. "We don't even have wolves in these woods. Unless I'm really a werecoyote."

Kate nodded, cracking a smile. "Right. So, we need to study this and find out if you're still contagious, and then trace it back to the source before anybody else in Marshall County turns into a werewolf."

"Assuming that hasn't already happened," Adam chimed in.

They both looked at him.

Kate and Dale exchanged a worried glance.

Kate frowned. "We had better do this fast," she said grimly.

Dale nodded. "It's a good thing this is kind of what we do."

Another moment passed.

Kate nodded slowly. "Right." She thought for a moment, and then, just like that, she had a plan. It was a simple one, but it would be fine, for now.

"Okay," she said, finally. "For now, our immediate problem is making sure nobody calls the police when first shift gets here. So, here's what we're going to do."

They both cocked their heads at her.

She looked around, nodding slowly. "Adam, you take Dale home. Clean yourselves up, and sort yourselves out. I'll stay here and clean this place up so nobody calls the cops." She looked up at him. "If anybody asks, we'll say Dale got sick and you took him home. We can just say you called me and I came to watch the station." She looked around, thinking that scenario through. "That works, right? We've got the station covered, and it gives you two a chance to think things through. I will… um… think of something for the door to the kitchenette."

They both nodded.

Kate lifted a finger and pointed delicately to Adam's furry forearms. "And, you might want to… ah… lose the wolf gloves."

Adam looked down at his hands, his eyes widening comically. "Oh! Right!" he said. He glared down in concentration at his arms. There was some assorted knuckle-popping, and his arms shrank down in size like molten plastic closing around a vacuum form. The fur thinned out and receded until there was nothing left, and then there was just plain old Adam, grinning like a moron at his own hands.

Kate shook her head. "I saw that and I still can't believe it." She looked at Dale.

Dale held his hands up. "I did it and I don't believe it." He was starting to look sick again.

Kate nodded. "Alright. The next shift gets in at eight. I'll come straight to Dale's and we'll figure out how the hell you got infected." She crossed her arms. "And, I'm going to want to see you transform. Completely."

Adam leered goofily at her. "Is that just an excuse to see me naked?"

Kate rolled her eyes. "God, Adam," she said. "It's good to see you're still the same horny idiot."

He stared at her for a moment, his eyes twinkling.

Dale shook his head. "I can't watch this," he grumbled. He began thumping his way toward the break room. "Need my bag. Get my keys. Wash my face. Then, get out of here." He staggered off across the wood floor and picked his way through the debris into the restroom. A second later, she heard water running loudly.

Kate watched Adam, who watched Dale with blissful, stupid devotion, and the look in the electrician's eyes was unquestionably… no. It couldn't be. Could it? After one night?

Impossible, there's no way Adam would have fallen this hard. And, yet…

Stranger things have happened, she thought, with a smile.

***

Dale took the stairs two at a time, pounding down them on his big booted feet. He needed to get outside.

Adam was right behind him. "Hey, Dale!" the big bald electrician protested. "Wait up!"

Dale hit the door hard, hard enough to make it bang against against the side of the building, and burst into the sunlight, gasping.

Unfortunately, outside wasn't any better. The scent of the forest, familiar but so much more significant now, like it had weight, roared over him like an ocean wave—pine cones and rotting leaves and tree sap and animal musk and even the gravel in the parking lot—and he staggered for a moment, trying to process all the information his senses were dumping into his brain. It was enough time for Adam to catch up behind him.

"Dale, what's the matter?" Adam asked, a concerned whine creeping into his voice. He gently grasped Dale's arm, stopping him in his tracks. "I can tell you're upset. What's the matter?"

He turned, and as soon as he lay eyes on Adam and his beautiful face, twisted into a grimace of concern, the ranger felt another surge of emotion. Bare your throat. Roll over. Go to him. Lick his face. Submit. Submit. Submit. SUBMIT. He snapped his eyes shut, clamping his meaty hands over his temples. The instincts welled up painfully inside him, and just as he was about to scream he felt Adam's arms around him, and then it all went quiet.

The big idiot squeezed his shoulders, and to Dale it felt like Adam was pushing the madness right out of him.

He opened his eyes and blinked, surprised. Suddenly, he felt okay again. Inches away from him, Adam smiled gorgeously.

Dale felt dread drop into his stomach.

He had to stop this now, before it got too far.

"Get off me," he growled.

Adam stared at him, his brow furrowing unhappily, and Dale shook his head. He bit his lip, fighting the urge to cower submissively. It would be better in the long run. He couldn't let this go on any further. Adam was young, and smart, and charismatic. He was going places, and Dale would just drag him down.

Dale pulled away and walked toward his truck. "This is where we part ways, Chaney," he snapped over his shoulder.

Adam stared back at him, shocked and hurt.

Swallowing hard, fumbling with his keys, Dale retreated to the far side of his truck and unlocked the driver's side door.

Adam just stood there.

Dale glanced back at him. He frowned pitifully.Swallowing a whimper, Dale set his face in an angry glare. "I mean it, Chaney!" he snapped. "I'm going home. I suggest you do the same."

The big man just stared at him. He wasn't going to leave, Dale knew, on a fundamental level. Dale didn't want him to leave, either, which somehow made it all worse.

Instead, Adam just watched him.

It was making him crazy.

"What's the matter with you, Chaney?!" he snarled.

Adam cocked his head. "You know… it's weird. Before we changed, I thought you were just an asshole," he said, solemnly. "But, now all I see is… fear."

Dale stared at him, open-mouthed, and now he got so mad he began shaking.

Adam watched him. "It's like… I can see your emotions now. I can smell them." He leaned forward. "You just look scared to me, Dale."

Dale grit his teeth, and he was so mad he couldn't even get any words out. How dare he, this shitty little kid. He knew nothing.

Adam frowned. "Hey, c'mon," he said, starting to creep around to Dale's side of the truck. He looked upset. "I know you're afraid, and I think you're afraid of me, but I can't…" His voice hitched for a moment. "I can't tell why." He grimaced, setting his jaw, and in that moment Dale could see a great and profound sadness.

Dale stared at him, and it was like all the anger drained out of him in one long, fast river, pouring out of him, until there was nothing left.

"Are you afraid of me?" Adam asked, softly.

Dale had to look away. He was tired and still felt sick and he wasn't right in the head. He felt his eyes start to tear up and he grit his teeth, clenching his hands into fists. "Adam, don't you get it?" he asked, wearily. "It doesn't matter. None of this matters." He took a deep breath. "What happened up there… that wasn't us. Those were just… animals." He swallowed, feeling hot, and looked hesitantly back up at the electrician. He was such a nice kid. "We changed, Adam. But, then… we changed back." He suddenly felt very tired.

Adam stared thoughtfully back at him, and then quietly shook his head. "You're wrong, Dale," he said, quietly. "We're wolves now." He nodded definitively. "I feel it. I know you do, too. We're different, now. Both of us."

Dale opened his mouth to argue, but he did not have a rebuttal for that, so he just let out a frustrated grunt and shut his mouth.

The big man came toward him, and Dale felt himself shrink against the side of the truck.

Adam cracked a warm lopsided smile, and pressed gently up against the ranger. He put one hand behind the small of Dale's back and the other hand on the back of the ranger's neck. Dale's head started swimming with his scent immediately.

"And, you don't have to be afraid of me. I would never hurt you." He set his jaw in determination. "And, I'm not going to leave you, either."

Dale stared at him, and let out a long, sad sigh. "Yeah, you will."

Adam snorted in his ear. "Some ranger you are."

Dale stared at him. He felt himself getting angry again. "What the hell's that supposed to mean?!" he demanded.

Adam grinned down at him. "How long do wolves mate for, Dale?"

The ranger stared at him, and then he felt his face getting hot. Adam grinned down at him, and finally he had to look away, blushing.

Finally, he was able to speak. "Don't push your luck, Chaney," he grumbled.

Adam laughed, deep and loud, and Dale felt himself resisting the urge to squirm in happiness at the reaction. It filled his heart, and after a moment he couldn't help but smile, too.

He leaned forward, and Adam swept him up into a big bear hug with his oversized arms. He squeezed Dale and nuzzled his right ear. "Hey, man. Relax," Adam rumbled into his ear. "I got you."

Dale swallowed, and let out a long, shaky sigh.

They stood there silently, for a long moment.

Adam finally angled his head and kissed Dale's forehead. "Do you really want me to leave?" he asked, softly.

Dale sighed. "No," he admitted, grunting unhappily.

Adam grinned. "Good. Because I'm not going anywhere." He leaned down to kiss him on the mouth, and in that moment of warm, wet contact, Dale felt his resolve completely crumble. They broke the kiss, and he rested his head against Adam's chest, and just stayed there.

He was still standing against Adam's chest a full minute later when he heard crunching on the gravel behind Adam. Dale felt so sleepy and relaxed in the bigger man's arms that it took him a moment to register. He blinked in mild surprise.

They slowly separated. Kate had come down the steps into the sunlight. For the first time Dale noticed her car standing in the middle of the lot with its driver's door hanging open, the engine quietly idling. He grimaced.

Adam apparently had the same thought. "Sorry if we scared you," he rumbled.

Kate smiled tiredly. "It's fine, you guys. I would say the concern was… warranted. I just gotta pull this into a parking space. You guys should get going, though. Tim gets in early sometimes." She climbed into her SUV and pulled the door shut. The window slid silently down a moment later. "I'll see you around eight, okay?"

Adam nodded. He turned back to Dale. "Where we going. Your place?" he asked. He headed for the passenger door of Dale's truck.

Dale nodded. Still unsure of what was going on in his own head, he climbed behind the wheel of his truck. As long as their little pack was together, he knew he would be okay.

He let out a shaky breath. God. What a weird thought. But, when was the last time he had felt like anything would be okay? At least this new feeling, however bizarre, was not unwelcome.

Adam opened the passenger door and climbed up into the truck. It creaked under his weight. "Hey," he said, turning.

Dale looked up at the grinning electrician.

Adam stared at him. "Are you glad I stayed last night?" he said, smugly.

"No," Dale grunted, though he couldn't keep the smile off his face. He started the engine.

He waved to Kate as they pulled out of the parking lot. In the seat next to him, his big lug of a werewolf boyfriend stretched his arms over his head and yawned out the window.

Despite himself, Dale smiled.

It was going to be a beautiful day.

About the Author:

Bill Siracusa—UnstableBill on social media—is a premier producer in a category that can only be described as "Adventure Porn." He owes a great debt to his editor, agent, and artist for translating that work into something that makes one bit of sense.

Bill lives in the Chicago suburbs with his husband, proving at last that hyenas can be (kind of) domesticated. He has previously been published in a sprinkling of anthologies and is ecstatic to be presenting his first solo endeavor.

About the Artist:

Skye is a full-time freelance dark artist who has been drawing for their whole life. They have a profound love of magic, adventure, and full moons. Skye lives in a quiet cemetery in the middle of a haunted forest with their fiancée. While they've been a part of other projects, this is their first published art deal.

You can find them on Twitter @ skyebluew0lf or support them on Patreon @SKY3~

About the Editor:

Khren Phyros is a freelance editor and avid fan of furry literature. He grew up down in the bayous of south Louisiana, but is currently living with his mate Rip K. and hoping to immigrate to Canada someday.

Overnight Shift is his first professional editing job, but he's done various informal editing for friends and family over the years. Hopefully, those reading this and any future stories he edits enjoy and appreciate all the hard work that the authors, artists, editors, and publishers all put into making a quality product for everyone to read!